All About Johnnie Jones

Carolyn Verhoeff

Contents

ALL ABOUT
JOHNNIE JONES

BY

Carolyn Verhoeff

These stories have been written with but one object, to give

pleasure to little children, while helping them to realize,

in so far as they are able, the highest ideals of childhood.

CAROLYN VERHOEFF

INTRODUCTION

It gives me sincere pleasure to introduce to mothers and kindergartners a pioneer writer in the unexplored field of simple, realistic stories for little children. Miss Verhoeff is a trained kindergartner who has brought to her profession a college training as well as a true devotion to children.

It was in one of the free kindergartens situated in the less fortunate localities of Louisville that the stories of Johnnie Jones came into being, and grew in response to the demand of the little ones for stories about real children.

In the beautiful world of fairy-lore we have a rich and splendidly exploited field of immortal literature. The old, old stories of fairies and elves, of giants and dwarfs, of genii, princes, and knights with their wonder-working wands, rings and swords, will never grow threadbare; while the spiritual, artistic and literary value of these stories in the life of child-imagination can never be overestimated. Enchanting and valuable as they are, however, they should not blind us to the need for standard realistic stories of equal literary and poetic merit.

A child needs not only the touch of the wonder-working wand which transports him to a land of fascinating unrealities, but also the artistic story which reflects the every-day experiences of real life; artistic in that it touches these daily experiences with an idealism revealing the significance and beauty of that which the jaded taste of the adult designates as "commonplace." That all children crave the story which is, or might be, true is evidenced by the expression of their faces when their inevitable question, "is it really true?" or "did it really happen?" is answered in the affirmative.

Perhaps some of us can recall the pleasure derived from old-fashioned school readers of an earlier day. With all their faults they at least did not overlook the value of standard realistic stories. In these readers was found the very moral story of the boy who won the day because of his forethought in providing an extra piece of whipcord. There was also "Meddlesome Matty," and the honest office-boy, the heroic lad of Holland, and the story of the newly liberated prisoner who bought a cage full of captive birds and set them free. These and many others still persist in memory, and point with unerring aim to standards of human behavior under conditions which are both possible and probable. In spite of their imperfections and stern morality these stories were valuable because they recited the fundamental events of human and animal existence, in relations which revealed the inevitable law of cause and effect, and the ethical and poetic significance of man's relation to all life.

As soon as children begin to realize the distinction between the world of make-believe and the world of actuality, or, as one small boy expressed it, "what I can see with my eyes shut, and what I can see when I open them," they are fascinated with stories of real life, of "when Father was a little boy," or "when Mother was a little girl," or "when you were a tiny baby." This demand of the child for realistic stories is the expression of a real want which should be satisfied with good literature.

Before children are enabled by their experience to discriminate between the imaginary and the actual world, they make no distinction between the story of real life and the fairy tale. During this early period a story relating the most ordinary events of every-day life is accepted in the same spirit, and may provoke as much or as little wonder, as the story dealing with the most marvelous happenings of the supernatural world. For to the child at this stage of development it is no more wonderful that trees and animals should converse in the language of men than that a little boy should do so. Until children learn that, as a matter of fact, plants and animals do not participate in all of the human activities, they regard as perfectly natural stories in which such participation is taken for granted. On the other hand a realistic story representing some of the most universal aspects of human existence may provoke surprise as the child discovers that his own experiences are common to many other lives and homes. This was evidenced by the remark of a small boy who, at the end of a story relating the necessary sequence of activities common to the countless thousands of heroic mothers, washing and ironing the family linen, waggishly shook his finger at the narrator, and with a beaming smile, said: "Now you know that it is _my_ Ma and Tootsie you are telling about!" John had not discovered the fact that the story which reflected the daily service of his beloved mother reflected equally well the service of thousands of other mothers. He saw only the personal experience in the common reality and recognized it with joy. When through similar stories of daily life a child learns to know that his experiences constitute the common lot, his first feeling of surprise gives place to a greater joy, and sympathy is born.

The stories of Johnnie Jones were not premeditated but grew in response to daily requests for "more about Johnnie Jones." They are the record of a most ordinary little boy, good as can be to-day, forgetting to obey to-morrow; a life history in which many other little lives are reflected in the old, old process of helping the child to adapt himself to the standards of society.

The ideal has been to deal with the ordinary events of daily life in a manner which will reveal their normal values to the child. There is the friendly policeman who finds the lost boy; the heroic fireman who comes to the rescue of the burning home; the little neighbor who would not play "fair;" the little boy who had to learn to roll his hoop, and to care for the typical baby brother who pulled his hair; there are the animals who entered into the joys and sorrows of the Jones family,-- altogether, very real animals, children, and "grown-ups," learning in common the lessons of social life.

The moral throughout is very pointed, and may be considered too obvious by many kindergartners, who do not feel the need of such insistence in their work. Mothers, however, with normal four-year-old boys who are likely to follow the music down the street and get lost, or who are equally liable to fall in the pond because they forget to obey Father, will find a strange necessity for pointing the moral in no uncertain tone.

The stories are so arranged that they may be read singly or as a serial.

I am sure the author will feel more than repaid if this little collection paves the way for more and better standard stories of reality, that our little children may not only revel in the events of a delightfully impossible world, but may also feel the thrill of heroism and poetry bound up in the common service of mother and father, of servants and neighbors, and find the threads of gold which may be woven into the warp and woof of daily intercourse with other little children who possess a common stock of privileges and duties, joys and sorrows.

PATTY SMITH HILL.
Louisville, Kentucky.

Johnnie Jones and the Cookie

One day, when Johnnie Jones was a wee little boy, only three years old, Mother came home from down town. Johnnie Jones ran to meet her. "Mother dear, didn't you bring me something?" he asked. "Yes, indeed," answered Mother, and she gave him something tied up in a paper bag. "Be careful," she told him, "or it will break."

So Johnnie Jones was careful as he untied the string and opened the bag. When he saw what was inside he was glad he had not broken it, for it was a round yellow cookie with a hole in the centre.

"Thank you, Mother," said Johnnie Jones, and he rolled on his back and kicked up his heels, which meant that he was happy. Then he sat up and began to eat his cookie. It was very good, and tasted as if it had molasses in it, Johnnie Jones said. But by and by, after he had been taking a great many bites, there wasn't any of the cookie left in his hand, because he had eaten it, every bit. Johnnie Jones looked at his hand where the cookie had been, and then he began to cry.

"Oh, dear me," exclaimed Mother, "what is troubling my little boy?"

"I want my cookie," cried Johnnie Jones.

"Where is your cookie?" asked Mother.

"I ate it," said Johnnie Jones.

"If you have eaten it, then it is all gone," Mother told him.

"But I want it! I want my cookie!" wailed Johnnie Jones.

"To-morrow I'll buy you another just like it," Mother promised.

"I don't want another just like it, I want my own cookie with a hole in the middle," and the tears came faster and faster.

"But, little boy," Mother said, "nobody in all the world, nor Father nor Mother nor Johnnie Jones, can eat a cookie and yet have it."

Johnnie Jones continued to cry, so Mother brought him some brown paper, a pair of scissors, and a pencil.

"See here, dear," she said, "I can't give you the cookie you ate, but you may make a picture that will look very much like it."

Then Johnnie Jones ceased crying, and Mother showed him how to fold and cut the paper until it was like the cookie, with a hole in the centre. They pasted it on cardboard and placed it upon the mantel.

"Thank you, Mother," said Johnnie Jones, "but I don't like it so well as my real cookie because I can't eat it."

"If you could eat it," Mother answered, "it would soon be gone, so the picture is better unless you are hungry."

And Johnnie Jones thought so too.

After that day he never again cried for a cookie when he had eaten it, nor for a toy when he had destroyed it, because he had discovered that crying could never bring back what was gone.

When Johnnie Jones Was Lost

Johnnie Jones was lost, completely lost. He looked up the street, he looked down the street, and then he looked across the street, but not one of the houses was his home. Johnnie Jones did not like being lost. He had not seen his mother for a very long time, not since she had left him in the yard at play after they had returned from market. He had been swinging on the front gate, when, suddenly, he heard the sound of music, and saw several people running down the street.

"Everyone must have forgotten to tell me that there was a circus," he said to himself. "I think I had better go see."

Now Johnnie Jones was never allowed to leave the yard unless an older person was with him, but he did not think of that, as he opened the gate and ran out on the street to follow the gathering crowd.

When he reached the first corner everyone was hurrying on to the next, and Johnnie Jones hurried on, too. Of course, however, he could not run as fast as older people, and very soon he was passed by the crowd. Then, when he could no longer hear the music, he looked about him and knew that he was lost.

He was sorry that he had gone away from home. He thought it must be about lunch time and he was very hungry. Then he remembered that this was the day Mother had promised to take him to the park. He would have cried, had he not been a brave little lad, and had he not known that a boy almost four is too old to cry, unless he is actually hurt.

He sat down on the curbstone, and wished and wished that some one would come to find him.

After a while he saw a policeman coming towards him from across the street. He was a very tall policeman, but Johnnie Jones decided to speak to him. His mother had often told him that policemen always take care of people, and help them whenever they can. So he tipped his hat politely, and said, "Please, Mr. Policeman, will you find me? Because I'm lost."

The policeman smiled down at Johnnie Jones until Johnnie Jones smiled up at the policeman and forgot what a little boy he was. Then the officer lifted him up in his strong arms, and asked him his name. Johnnie Jones could tell him his name, but he could not tell him which way he had come from home, so they decided to go to the nearest drug-store and find the number of the house.

The policeman began to tell him stories about his own little boy whose name was Johnnie Green, and Johnnie Jones was so interested that he forgot to be tired. Just before they reached the drug-store Johnnie Jones heard a dog barking. He looked around, and there was the very dog that lived next door to him and played with him every day.

"Oh!" he said, "I know that dog! He is Max, and he can find the way home." "You'll take me home, won't you, Max?" he asked the dog, who was so glad to see his little neighbor that he was trying his best to kiss him on the face.

"All right," the big policeman said, "but I'll come too, so I shall know where you live if you are ever lost again."

Max wagged his tail and began to trot home. Johnnie Jones trotted after Max, and the policeman after Johnnie Jones. It was not very long before they could see the house, and there was Mother standing at the gate, looking up the street, and down the street, and across the street, for her little boy. When she saw him she ran to meet him and clasped him in her arms.

"Mother dear," said Johnnie Jones, "I was lost, and the policeman found me, and then Max found us both, and I shall never again go to see a circus by myself."

Mother told him that the band of music he had heard did not belong to a circus, but was the Citizen's Band on its way to the park, and that, since so much time had passed while Johnnie Jones was lost, it was too late for him to go to the park that day. Of course the little boy was sorry to miss the treat, but he was very glad to be at home once more.

Mother shook hands with the policeman, and thanked him for being kind to her boy. As soon as he had gone, she and Johnnie Jones went into the house for their lunch, and, afterwards, the little fellow was so tired that he fell asleep in Mother's lap and dreamed that he was a tall policeman finding lost boys.

Mother's Story of the Princess and Her Pigeon

"Mother," asked Johnnie Jones, "what is a carrier pigeon?"

"A pigeon which is trained to carry messages from one place to another," Mother answered. "In the olden times, as there were no trains, or steamboats, or postmen, or telegraph offices, people would very often take pigeons with them when they started off on a long journey. As soon as they reached their journey's end they would write a letter to the family so far away, tie it to a pigeon, and release him. Then the pigeon would fly away home with the message."

"Once, in that olden time, there lived a beautiful princess whom her father and mother, the king and queen, decided to send away on a visit to her grandmother. They gave her a milk-white pony to ride, and sent many servants to take care of her. Now this princess had a pet pigeon which she loved very dearly, and which she insisted upon taking with her, though the queen was afraid it might prove troublesome on so long a journey. The princess knew it would be a comfort to her, however, so she was allowed to tie it to her saddle before she bade her parents good-by, and started off.

"The princess had never been away from home before, and was very much interested in everything she saw. She and her companions had to travel through a great forest, and only the guides knew the way. One night everyone was lying fast asleep on the ground in the thick woods, except the princess, who was wide awake in her tent. At last she wearied of lying there alone, so she rose, dressed herself, and went out into the woods, carrying the pigeon in her arms.

"The moon was shining as bright as day, and the little girl went for a walk. She was thinking of the father and mother at home, and did not notice very carefully the direction in which she was wandering. After a while she grew tired and turned back. Then she became frightened because she could not see her tent, and could not remember which way she had come. She called for her servants, but could make no one hear her. She ran this way and that in the forest, but seemed only to go further and further away from the camp. At last, very tired, she lay down on the ground and cried herself to sleep.

"Next morning when the servants awoke they were very much alarmed to discover that the princess had left her tent. They spent several days seeking her in the forest, but not a trace of her could they find. Then they went back to inform the king and queen, who were sad indeed to hear such news. The king himself rode off to search in the forest, but even he could not find the little maid.

"Meanwhile the princess had been wandering further and further away into the great forest, with the pigeon tied to her arm. Fortunately, she had brought with her a small basket full of lunch, which had been left by her bed in case she should be hungry during the night. That was soon gone, however, and then she had a hard time finding enough to eat. But here and there she discovered wild berries, she drank water from the clear, cold springs, and at night she found a comfortable, fragrant bed under the pine trees, or in places where the grass was long and soft. Sometimes wild animals came out, and looked at the little girl, but they did not harm her.

"At last, the third day, she came to a large palace in the woods. Oh! how happy she was. A prince met her at the door, invited her in, and gave her delicious food and beautiful clothes. When she was rested after her long journey, she told the prince who she was, and the reason for her being alone in the forest, and begged him to send her home. The prince was sorry for the little princess, but he was lonely in such a large palace, so he asked her to live there with him. He was very kind to her, but the princess wanted only to go home to be with her father and mother.

"'Your palace is larger and more beautiful than my father's house,' she told him, 'but I love my own home best, and I want to go back this very day.'

"The prince was sorrowful when he heard what the little girl said; but, hoping she might learn to care for his palace after a while, he gave her a beautiful room filled with lovely things, and did everything he could think of to make her happy.

"The little princess did try to be happy, but it was not possible. Every evening she watched the birds fly back to their nests and she wished that she, too, had wings and could fly away home. The pigeon was as homesick as she. He would not eat, and pulled at the cord all the time, trying to free himself. Finally the little princess decided to let him fly away. 'Perhaps he can find his way home,' she thought; 'anyway I shall let him try.'

"She wrote a letter to her father and mother, telling them where she was, tied it under the pigeon's wing, and set him free. He flapped his wings joyfully and flew out of the window high up in the air. Round and round he circled, until in his own way he learned that the west was to the right of him, the east to the left, the north was back of him, and the south straight ahead. Then he started off like an arrow shot from a bow, for home was there in the south.

"The little princess was more homesick than ever, left all alone.

"Meantime the pigeon flew very swiftly, sometimes as fast as a train can go. No one can tell you how he knew the way, but he flew straight back through the woods, and after a while reached the pigeon house just outside the palace gate. Some of the servants who saw him fly in with the note, caught him and carried him to the king. The king and queen read the letter with great joy when they saw it had been written by their little daughter, and all the people in the palace were happy to know that the princess was safe and well.

"The pigeon flew back to the pigeon house. 'Coo, coo, coo,' he said to all the other pigeons, 'home is the best place in the world.'

"The king ordered the fastest horses in the land, and he and the queen rode off at once to find their little daughter. One day she saw them coming. She clapped her hands with joy and ran to meet them. The king and queen were as happy as she, and after they had greeted her, and bade the prince good-by, they all three rode away home. The princess sat in front of her father on his horse, because he could not bear to have her out of his arms. After travelling back through the forest they reached the palace at last.

"'Home is the best place in the world,' said the happy little princess.

"'Home is the best place in the world,' cooed the happy little pigeon."

Johnnie Jones lay back in Mother's arms. "I think so too," he said, "I like Grandma's house and Auntie's house, but home is best of all."

Johnnie Jones and the Squirrel

"Come," said Mother, "leave your toys now, and bathe your face and hands, for it is time to go down town to buy your winter coat."

"Oh! Mother, I don't want to go down town," answered Johnnie Jones, "because I think Sammy Smith is coming over to play with my new engine this afternoon."

"But what will you do when the weather grows cold and you have no warm coat to wear? I shall be too busy to go with you to-morrow."

"It's so warm to-day, Mother, I don't think it will grow cold very soon, and anyway, I don't want to go down town."

Mother answered: "I know it will be cold soon, perhaps to-morrow, for the wind is beginning to blow from the north. Come as soon as you can, I have much to do and can't wait for you very long."

Then Johnnie Jones behaved like a silly little boy, although he was four years old, quite old enough to know better. He fussed and fumed until Mother said: "I am sorry, but I can't wait any longer." She went on down town and left Johnnie Jones.

Sammy Smith did not come over to play after all, because he had gone shopping with his mother. Johnnie Jones soon grew tired of playing alone and wished he had not been so foolish.

That night the north wind blew and blew, so that, next morning, it was very cold when Johnnie Jones awoke. Of course he could not go to kindergarten nor out to play, because he had no heavy coat to wear. He begged his mother to wrap him in a shawl, and take him down town in the carriage, but she was too busy. So poor little Johnnie Jones had to stay in the house all day.

That evening when it was time for his story, Mother said: "I shall have to tell you the story of the foolish squirrel, because you reminded me of him to-day."

This is the story.

Once upon a time, there lived in the woods a little squirrel whose name was Silver. All summer long he played about with the other squirrels and had a very good time indeed. Then, by and by, the days began to grow shorter and cooler. The trees began to drop their brightly colored leaves and their nuts, and the soft green grass turned brown. The wise old mother squirrels knew what these things meant, and they said to all the young ones:

"Winter is coming, so hurry away,   You have no longer time to play. Gather the nuts with all your might   Before the ground with snow is white. When winter comes there's naught to eat   Except the roots and nuts so sweet, Which you must gather in the fall. So frisk away and store them all."

The squirrels, large and small, went to work. They found holes in the trees and old logs in which to hide their winter provisions, and they scampered away to find their favorite food.

All except little Silver. He said to himself: "Humph! I don't believe winter is coming so very soon, and besides, I'd rather just play, and eat the nuts, than work as these other squirrels are doing."

So he played as he had all summer long, and he kept so warm frisking about in the sunshine that he did not realize how short and cold the days were growing.

At last winter really came. Oh! how cold it was then. Silver said: "Perhaps I had better begin gathering some nuts for winter." But very few nuts could he find, not nearly enough to store away. The other squirrels, and the people who lived near the woods, had been working while he was playing, and had gathered in the harvest.

Poor little Silver did not know what to do. Winter was here and he had no provisions. He went to all the other squirrels and begged for some of their nuts. They only said: "You were playing while we were working, now you must work while we rest and eat."

Then Silver was sorry he had not obeyed the wise old squirrels and he told himself that, next year, he would surely begin early to prepare for winter. But there might not have been a "next year" for Silver, if a little boy had not found him in the woods and taken him home to keep and feed until the spring-time.

Johnnie Jones and the Peach Preserves

Everyone knows that people prepare for winter during the summer and fall. (Bees and squirrels and caterpillars do, too.) Almost everybody lays in the coal and kindling wood for the winter fires while the weather is still warm, and buys warm clothing before it is time to wear it.

In the summer, farmers cut the long grass, and after it has been dried by the sun, store it in the barns for the cows and horses to eat in the winter. In the summer and the autumn, people do not eat all the berries, and grapes, and pears and peaches; some they make into preserves and jelly for the winter.

Mrs. Jones could make delicious preserves. She enjoyed making it and Johnnie Jones liked to help her. He could really help a great deal because he was a careful little boy. Every member of the Jones family liked peach preserves better than any other kind, therefore Mother usually made enough of it to fill many jars. This year, however, she had been so busy that she did not start her preserving very early, and when she was ready to begin, she found it was too late to buy many good peaches. She bought a few, though, and preserved them with Johnnie Jones's help.

When the preserves was made. Mother had enough to fill four glass jars. "Not very much," she told Johnnie Jones, "but there is one jar for Father, one for you and one for me, and then one more for company." She left the jars on the kitchen table while she went upstairs to change her dress.

Johnnie Jones ran out into the yard to play. He saw Sammy Smith, Elizabeth, and Ned across the street, and called them. "I want to show you something," he said.

When they came, he led them to the kitchen and showed them the preserves.

"I should like to have some of it," said Ned,--"may I?"

"We made it to use in the winter," Johnnie Jones explained, "when there isn't any fresh fruit."

"I'd like some now on a piece of bread." Ned insisted.

"You said one jar of preserves was yours; give us each a taste," begged Sammy Smith.

"I don't think Mother meant that I might eat it whenever I wanted it," Johnnie Jones answered. "But perhaps she wouldn't care if we should each take a taste," he added.

Now Johnnie Jones knew he was not allowed to eat between meals, but the preserves did have an attractive appearance, and he thought that just one taste would not matter.

The top of the jar had not yet been sealed, so it came off very easily. Johnnie Jones gave a piece of bread, with a very little of the preserves, to each child, and took some for himself.

"It is good!" Ned exclaimed. "Give us some more, Johnnie Jones, your mother won't care."

Johnnie Jones was afraid Mother would care, but he liked the preserves very much, and besides, he enjoyed giving it to the children, so he gave them each a little more and again took some for himself. It was curious that the more they had the more they wanted, and after each one had been given "just a little more," several times, the large jar was nearly empty.

"We may as well finish it," said Ned, So they did. Then the children went home and left Johnnie Jones alone in the kitchen with the empty jar.

Johnnie Jones was unable to eat his supper that evening. Mother asked him what was the matter, and he told her. She was very sorry.

"Oh! little son," she said, "all your life I have been able to trust you, and I did not think you would touch the preserves, when I left the jars on the table. Say you are sorry, dear, and that such a thing shall never happen again. For wouldn't it be dreadful if I should be obliged to lock up everything I can't let you have?"

Johnnie Jones was very sorry indeed, but he answered: "You said that one jar was mine."

"So I did," Mother answered; "but I had no idea that you would want to use it all at one time, or between meals, or before the winter-time. Since you have had all your share to-day, you will, of course, expect no more next winter, when Father and I have ours."

Just then, Johnnie Jones thought he would never wish for peach preserves again, for he had eaten too much and felt uncomfortable; but probably he changed his mind in the winter, and regretted that his share was all gone.

Sammy Smith, Elizabeth and Ned came to see Mrs. Jones next day, told her they were sorry they had begged for the preserves, and asked her to excuse them, which of course she did.

Mother was glad to find that it would be unnecessary to lock up forbidden things after all, for Johnnie Jones liked to have her trust him, and showed her that she could.

How the Children Helped Tom and Sarah

Most of the houses on Park street, where the Jones family lived, were large and pretty, but there was one house that was very small and ugly. It had been unoccupied for a long time, when one day, Sarah and Tom Watson, with their father and mother, moved in. The little brother and sister were such agreeable children, that they were soon known and loved by all their small neighbors.

One morning, when Johnnie Jones was passing the ugly little house, he saw Sarah and Tom standing at the gate with an unhappy expression on their faces, usually so bright. Johnnie Jones stopped and asked them what was the trouble.

"We don't know what to do," answered Tom. "A friend of Father's promised to send him a load of coal to-day. It may come any minute and Father is too busy to put it into the coal-house. Mother can't attend to it because she must finish some sewing for a lady, so there is no one but Sarah and me. We are afraid we can't put it all away before night, and if it isn't locked up in the coal-house this evening, something may happen to it while we are asleep, and then we shouldn't have any coal to keep us warm in the winter."

"Why don't you hire a man to put it away for you?" asked Johnnie Jones.

"We haven't money enough," Tom answered.

"I'd better go home and ask my mother what to do. She'll know," said Johnnie Jones.

"Well," Mother said, when she had heard of the children's difficulty, "Sarah and Tom need friends to help them, so why don't you, in your overalls, and Ned, Susie, and the other children in theirs, take your wagons and wheelbarrows, and spend the afternoon helping with the coal? A dozen pairs of hands, even if they are small, can accomplish a great deal of work."

Mother sent her hired man to see that the coal-house was ready for the coal, while Johnnie Jones hurried off to collect the children.

The boys and girls dressed in their overalls hastened to the small brown house. There they found Sarah and Tom as busy as bees, and very happy to welcome the children gathered to help them. Such a merry time as they had! Some of the children played that they were strong horses, and drew the wagons, which the others loaded at the gate and unloaded at the coal-house door. Very soon the play drivers looked like real drivers of coal-carts for they were covered with coal-soot from their heads to their feet. All of the children, too, worked quite as hard as any real horses, or any real men, and after a while, before dark, the load of coal was safe in the coal-house. Then the children ran home for a much-needed bath.

Meantime Mrs. Watson had been sewing all the day long, and in the evening, when it was time to go home, she felt very tired. All day she had worried about the coal, wondering how she could attend to it that night. She knew that her children would try to help, but she did not expect very much from them because their hands were so small. As she walked home she thought, and thought, trying to decide what was best to do.

At last she came near the ugly little house, and then she was greatly surprised, for Sarah and Tom, neat and clean, were swinging on the gate, the pavement was nicely swept, and there was no sign of any coal.

"Didn't the coal come?" she asked the children.

"Yes," they answered joyfully, "and it is in the coal-house."

She could scarcely believe them, but they said: "Come and see."

When she saw that the coal was really there, locked away for the winter in the shed, she was almost too surprised and pleased to speak.

At last she asked the delighted children whether the fairies had come to their aid. "No," they answered, "but all the children in the neighborhood did, and we had such a good time that it was almost the same as giving a party."

"The children were very kind," Mrs. Watson said, when she had heard all about the happy afternoon. "We could not have managed the coal without their assistance, and some day we must try to help them."

Johnnie Jones's Story of the Stars

The stars were just beginning to show themselves in the dark blue sky, when Mother and Johnnie Jones sat down by the window to watch for Father. Mother and Johnnie Jones loved the stars. Almost every evening they sat and looked up at them. Sometimes they tried to count them, but they never could, because there were so very many. Often, too, they could see the bright, round moon. Johnnie Jones said that a queer, fat little man lived in the moon, who winked and bowed whenever little boys looked at him. To be polite, Johnnie Jones always returned the winks and bows. But this night there was no moon, just the little stars were appearing, and twinkling as fast as they could.

"Mother," said Johnnie Jones, "I'll tell you a story all my own, about the shining stars."

"I'd like very much to hear it," Mother answered.

"Once upon a time, oh! such a very long time ago that it must have been before you were born, Mother dear, all the stars fell down from the sky. I think it was the wind that blew and blew until they became loose. They fell down whirling and twirling just like the snow flakes, except that they weren't cold and white, but all bright and shining. They were so beautiful that the people looked out of their windows and wished the stars would never stop raining down from the sky."

"Is that all the story?" asked Mother, much interested.

"No, there is another part," said Johnnie Jones. "When all the stars had fallen down to the ground, what do you suppose they really were?"

"I can't imagine," Mother answered.

"Why, Mother, they were beautiful little flowers all different colors. Some were red, some were yellow, and some were purple violets. They began to grow, and nobody gathered any, for they were so pretty there on the ground."

"But," asked Mother, "when it was night time again, what did the poor people do without any stars to shine in the sky?"

"Don't you see," Johnnie Jones explained, "when the stars fell down they left little holes in the sky, and the light behind shone through and seemed just like the stars."

"I think that is a beautiful story," and Mother thanked him with a kiss, before they ran down-stairs to meet Father coming home.

Johnnie Jones and Jack

One day, when Johnnie Jones was playing in his front yard, he heard the yelping of a dog. He ran to the gate, and saw, lying in the street, a poor little puppy which had been hurt by a wagon, or perhaps, an automobile.

"You may come home with me, you poor little thing," Johnnie Jones told the dog. "My mother will rub salve on you and make you well. Come on."

But the poor little puppy couldn't walk. Johnnie Jones picked him up, and attempted to carry him to the house. The puppy was so heavy, however, that Johnnie Jones was obliged to put him down and take him up again, three times, before he reached the side door. He called to Mother to come down.

"But, little son," she said, "we can't keep a strange dog. We shall have to let him run away."

"Oh, Mother, he's hurt, and I am sure he's hungry, so don't you think we shall have to keep him?"

Of course, as soon as Mother understood that the puppy was hurt, she knew that it would be necessary to keep him, at least until he was well again. She examined the little fellow and found that he was not badly injured, but was merely bruised and frightened. She and Johnnie Jones bathed and bandaged the poor little body, and when the puppy seemed to feel more comfortable, gave him a bowl of milk. He could not say "Thank you," but he wagged his tail, and kissed their hands, which meant "Thank you," so they agreed that he was a polite little dog,

"But where shall we keep him?" asked Mother. "I can't allow him in the house, he would gnaw the legs of the chairs and tables; all puppies do when they are cutting their teeth."

"Perhaps Father and I can build a doghouse," Johnnie Jones answered, and when Father came home they talked it over.

"Well," Father decided, "If the grocery man will give us a large box, we can line it, fill it with straw, and I'll cut a door in one end. That should make an excellent house for Mr. Doggie."

Johnnie Jones ran to the grocery-store as fast as he could run, and asked the grocery man to send down a large box. As soon as it came, Father cut the door, Johnnie Jones arranged the straw, and there was the house all ready for the dog.

Johnnie Jones named him Jack. Jack soon became well and strong, and because he was such a good dog, and because his owner could not be found, he was allowed to remain at Johnnie Jones's house. He wasn't a puppy very long. He grew and grew, until he was too large for his box, and had to sleep in the front hall of the Jones's house. He and Johnnie Jones loved each other dearly, and were almost always together. Mother used to say that they reminded her of Mary and her lamb, except that Jack was as black as coal.

You remember how Mary's lamb followed her to school one day, which was against the rule? Well, it was necessary to keep Jack in the closet every morning, until after Johnnie Jones had gone to kindergarten, because he always wanted to go with him. One morning the door was not fastened securely, and Jack was able to push it open. Then, before any one saw him, he ran out the gate, and followed Johnnie Jones. The little boy did not see him and did not know that Jack was just behind him as he entered the kindergarten room, until the children began to laugh and he turned around to see what was the matter. There stood Jack, wagging his tail with all his might.

The children begged Miss Page, the teacher, to let Jack spend the morning in kindergarten, and she said that she would try him. She was afraid, however, that he would not know how to behave. Johnnie Jones was a trifle late that morning, and the children were all ready to march to the circle. Jack followed his master as he marched to his place, and then sat down on the floor beside the little boy's chair.

Miss Page asked the children which one of them would like to stand in the centre of the circle and shake hands with the others, in turn, as they sang the good-morning song.

"Let Jack," said Johnnie Jones, "he can shake hands as well as anybody, and he is a visitor to-day."

Miss Page consented, and Johnnie Jones called Jack to the circle and offered him his hand. Jack at once gave him his paw. One by one the children came and shook Jack's paw. Everyone considered it great fun, and Jack enjoyed it also, though he could not laugh as the children did.

As soon as all the good-mornings had been sung, Miss Page started a game of ball. Now there was nothing that Jack liked better than playing with a ball, so he ran out on the circle barking, and jumped up on the boy who had the ball in his hand. The boy became frightened, not understanding what Jack wanted, and let the ball fall and roll away. Jack rushed after it, knocking down chairs and tables, spilling the blocks out of their boxes, and tearing paper chains to bits. At last he caught the ball in his mouth, brought it to Johnnie Jones, and began to jump and bark, begging the little boy to throw it.

Miss Page said that she was sorry, but Jack would have to go home. "He is a very good dog," she said, "but he does not behave well in kindergarten."

At that moment Sam, the hired man, came into the room. Mrs. Jones had missed Jack and sent Sam to find him. Jack was having a pleasant time and did not want to go home, but he knew how to obey, and, when Johnnie Jones commanded him to "go home," he turned slowly and walked out of the room.

So you see, Jack was turned out by the teacher, just as was Mary's lamb.

One bright day, when the ground was covered with snow, Father took Johnnie Jones for a ride on his sled. They had been around the block only twice when the clock struck two, and then it was time for Father to go to his office.

"Oh! dear," said Johnnie Jones, "now I'll have no one to pull my sled. I wish Jack could."

"Perhaps he can," Father answered. "When I come home to-night I'll make some sort of a harness for him, and then to-morrow we shall see what he can do."

That evening, with rope, straps, and Johnnie Jones's reins Father made a very good harness, and the next day he hitched Jack to the sled. At first Jack could not imagine what Father and Johnnie Jones wished him to do. He allowed himself to be hitched to the sled, but every time Johnnie Jones sat upon it, and said "Get up," Jack would jump about, and off would roll Johnnie Jones into the snow. Then Jack would bark as much as to say, "What are you trying to do, anyway?"

At last, after many trials, Father managed to hold Jack quiet until Johnnie Jones was seated firmly on the sled, clasping a side with each hand. Then Father, still keeping a tight hold of Jack, ran with him to the corner and back several times. At last Jack began to understand what was expected of him. The next day they tried again, and it was not long before Johnnie Jones could drive the big dog without Father's help. After a while Jack would even pull Johnnie Jones's sled to kindergarten each morning, and then draw the empty sled home, after Johnnie Jones had gone into the house. He certainly was a clever dog. It was no wonder Johnnie Jones loved him.

In the winter-time there was an excellent place for coasting in the park very near Johnnie Jones's house. There was a long, straight hill, and at the foot of it a long, straight pond, so that, with a good start, a child could coast from the top of the hill to the end of the pond. That is, of course, when there was snow and the pond was frozen over at the same time.

One afternoon Johnnie Jones started out with his sled and Jack ran along beside him.

"Don't try to coast across the pond to-day," called Father. "When I was passing I noticed that the ice was broken in several places."

"Then I'll coast on the other side of the hill," Johnnie Jones answered.

When he reached the park, however, he found two of the children coasting across the pond as usual. One of them, whose name was Ned, asked Johnnie Jones: "What's the matter with everybody to-day? Where are the other children?"

"I suppose their fathers wouldn't let them come," answered Johnnie Jones; "and you shouldn't coast across the pond. My father just told me that it isn't safe, because the ice is beginning to break."

"Oh! it is perfectly safe," Ned replied, "because we have been over it several times. The coasting is better fun to-day than ever before, and there are no children to block the way. Come and try it."

"I wish I might," Johnnie Jones answered. He sat on his sled and watched the older boys coast safely across, and run gaily back, waving their hands to him.

"Perhaps my father was mistaken." he said after a while. "I think I'll try it just once."

"There is one tolerably large hole," Ned warned him, "but it is on one side, and if you are careful you won't fall in."

"I'll be careful," answered Johnnie Jones; "you sit here and watch me."

He placed himself flat on his sled, and Ned gave him a push. Johnnie Jones was not quite five years old then, two years younger than Ned, and he could not guide his sled very well. When it went near the big hole, he could not turn it away. Then splash! Both Johnnie Jones and the sled plunged into the icy cold water.

The water was not very deep, but as Johnnie Jones struck it head foremost, and as the sled was on top of him, he might have found some trouble in forcing his way out, had it not been for Jack. That faithful friend was close beside his little master, and in just a few seconds had drawn him out of the water.

As soon as Ned and Sammy Smith saw what had happened, they hurried to the house and told Mr. Jones. He ran all the way to the pond, picked up the little wet, cold boy, and carried him home as quickly as possible.

Jack was wet and cold too, but he ran around so fast that he soon grew warm, then he crawled under the kitchen stove, where he stopped until he was dry. But Johnnie Jones had to go to bed, for several days, with a very bad cold.

He was sorry he had been disobedient, and asked Father please to excuse him that time. Father said he would not punish him, but that he was sorry to think his little boy did not trust his father.

"I do, Father," Johnnie Jones answered, "and after this I'll obey you, instead of minding little boys."

"Grown people generally know best," Father said.

After that, of course, Mother, Father and Johnnie Jones loved good old Jack more than ever, and were glad they had kept him when he first came to them a puppy, hurt and hungry.

Stiggins

Johnnie Jones's Aunt Jean owned a dog. His name was Stiggins, just Stiggins, for dogs need only one name, instead of the two or three that people have. Aunt Jean was accustomed to go to Lake Chautauqua every summer, far away from home. Stiggins liked to go with her, and was always afraid that he might be left behind, as had happened, once or twice. So, as soon as he saw Aunt Jean begin to make her preparations, he would spend all his time either following her about, or lying on her trunk.

Each time she started to pack she would first have to drive Stiggins into the yard. If she turned away, just for a few minutes, there he would be again, lying in a tray upon her best dresses, or her prettiest hats. Aunt Jean would scold and scold, but scolding was of no use.

At last, when the day came on which they were to begin their journey, and the trunks had been locked and sent away, Stiggins would run to the stable, jump into the carriage, and there he would stay until he and the family had reached the station.

But when it was time to board the train, Stiggins was most unhappy. He was forced to ride in the baggage car, all alone, and Stiggins liked company. He wished to ride in the sleeping car with Aunt Jean. Of course he could not, because he was only a dog, which was something that Stiggins had never quite understood. He would whimper, and run away, when the coachman attempted to lead him to his proper place, so usually, Aunt Jean had to take him, and to tie him, herself.

Stiggins disliked the long ride on the train and boat, but he was just the happiest dog in the world when at last he reached Chautauqua. When once he was there he had many fine times, bathing in the Lake, going off on long walks and drives with the family, and playing with the dogs.

The house in which Aunt Jean lived was very near the lake, and Stiggins liked to lie on the front porch and watch the children at play by the water's edge. One day, Harry and Sally were there with a small sail-boat attached to a string, which Harry held, as the boat sailed out on the water. Suddenly the string broke, and then there was nothing with which to draw the boat to land.

The children were quite small and did not know what to do. They asked a big boy to wade out and return the boat to them, but he was a lazy boy and told them to throw stones beyond the boat to make it come back of itself. They tried his plan, but were not strong enough to throw the stones very far, and the boat only floated further away.

All this time Stiggins had been lying on the porch watching the children. I am not sure whether he thought they were throwing stones for him to swim after, or whether he saw they were in trouble and wished to help them, but this is what he did. Without a word from anyone, he jumped up, trotted down to the water and waded in. The children and the big boy wondered what he meant to do. Stiggins himself seemed to know very well. He swam straight to the boat, caught it in his mouth, brought it to land, and dropped it at the children's feet. Then he trotted back to the porch.

Harry and Sally thought that Stiggins was the kindest and most polite dog they had ever seen, and the big boy was ashamed, because he thought that a dog had been kinder and more polite than he.

This story is as true as true can be. I know, because Aunt Jean saw the whole affair and she told me about it herself.

When Johnnie Jones was a Santa Claus

"I should think it would be exciting to be Santa Claus," said Johnnie Jones, "and fill children's stockings when they are asleep in bed. I should like very well to be his helper some time."

"You may be," Mother answered; "anyone who really wishes to be Santa's assistant, may be."

Johnnie Jones was surprised. "Well, I didn't know that," he said. "Please tell me how."

"Whenever people give Christmas presents to those they love, they are a sort of Santa Claus," Mother told him. "But this year you may be a real Santa Claus, if you like, with a real pack of toys, and you may fill some real stockings belonging to some real children, this coming Christmas Eve."

"Oh! Mother dear, tell me all about it, quick as a wink," begged Johnnie Jones, clapping his hands with delight.

"I thought you would be pleased," Mother answered. "Father knows of a large house in which ever so many children live who have never hung up their stockings. I suppose no one has thought to tell Santa Claus about them, and their fathers and mothers are very poor. Father and I want to make them have a bright, happy Christmas this year, and he has told them, each one, to be sure to hang up stockings on Christmas Eve for a Santa Claus to fill. If you like, you may be that Santa, and Father and I will be your assistants, and we'll go, all three of us, to the house at night when the children are fast asleep."

Johnnie Jones skipped joyfully about the room. "Shall we go in a sleigh with bells and reindeer?" he asked.

"We'll go in a sleigh if there is snow," Mother promised, "but I am afraid we shall have to use horses, and pretend they are reindeer."

Johnnie Jones was greatly excited. He asked Mother every question he could think of, and wished it were Christmas Eve that very minute. Mother told him be should be glad they still had several days before Christmas in which to make their preparations.

That same afternoon they went shopping. Johnnie Jones was allowed to select the toys for the children, and he chose enough drums and horses, wagons and cars, dolls and play-houses, dishes and tables, to fill four very large boxes. Next, they ordered the candy, pounds and pounds of it, and a big tree with ever so many candles for it. Last of all, they bought warm coats and shoes.

The next three days was a busy time for Johnnie Jones. After he had finished his gifts for the family, he went to work on the decorations for the tree. He made yards and yards of brightly colored paper chains, and many cornucopias. Every evening before his bed-time Mother and Father helped him.

At last the day before Christmas came. When Johnnie Jones awoke in the morning he was very much pleased to find the ground covered with snow. It was hard to wait until night, but he was busy all day, and the time passes quickly when one is busy.

After a very early supper Father, Mother and Johnnie Jones dressed themselves in their warmest clothing and heaviest wraps. By the time they were ready, there was the sleigh, drawn by two strong horses wearing many bells, standing before the house. It was quite a while before the toys, and candy, and ornaments, were safely packed in the sleigh, but at last all was in readiness, and away they went.

After a long, beautiful ride over the hard snow, with the moon and stars shining up in the sky, they reached the big house.

"Are all the children asleep?" Father asked two men who were waiting for them at the door.

The men answered yes, and Father whispered to Johnnie Jones: "We must be very quiet, Santa Claus, that we may not waken anybody."

They tiptoed carefully into the first room where several children were asleep in their beds.

"I see the stockings," whispered Johnnie Jones eagerly. "Give me my sack."

Father placed the heavy sack on the floor, and the little Santa and Mother filled the stockings with candy and nuts, oranges and tiny toys. As soon as Father had set up the tree in an empty room, he came back to help. It was the best kind of fun, but they had to be very quiet in order not to waken the children. Once Johnnie Jones couldn't help laughing aloud when a ridiculous old Jack popped out of the box in his hand. The laugh awoke a little boy, who sat up in bed and called out, "Hello! Is that you, Santa Claus?" They had to leave the room until he fell asleep again.

When all the stockings had been filled, the tree decorated, and the presents arranged under it, Father locked the door of that room so that no one should peep in before it was time. Little Santa Claus was so tired that he went to sleep in Father's arms on the way home, and when he was being carried to bed awoke only long enough to hang his own stocking by the fire-place.

The next morning he opened his eyes very early, as is the custom of children on Christmas Day. He looked for his stocking, first of all, wondering if Santa had filled it. Of course he had, with all the things that little boys like best.

Johnnie Jones was so happy over his presents, that he could scarcely take time to dress. At last Mother reminded him of those other children waiting so anxiously for their first Christmas tree. Johnnie Jones laid down his new toys immediately, and dressed himself as quickly as possible. Directly after breakfast they returned to the big house, this time on the street car.

Before they turned the corner on their way to the house, they heard the voices of the children, who were full of joy over the presents found in their stockings. Father went at once to the room he had locked up the night before, and lighted the candles on the tree. When all was ready he opened the door, and Johnnie Jones invited the children to enter.

They stood very quietly about the tree, not saying a word at first. It was so beautiful, and so different from anything they had ever seen, that it made them feel shy. But when Father called the children in turn, and Johnnie Jones gave to every one a warm coat, a new pair of shoes, and a splendid toy, they found their tongues, and made such a noise as you never heard.

They had to dress themselves in the coats and shoes, and they had to show each other their toys. Some of them had to turn somersaults, and all of them had to make a great noise just to express their joy.

But happiest of all those happy children was little Johnnie Jones.

All too soon, Father, Mother and Johnnie Jones had to leave, so that they might reach Grandmother's house in time for dinner. When they were again on the car, the little boy began to talk of the good time they had had.

"I'd like to be a Santa Claus every year," he said.

"Then save your pennies," Mother answered, "until next Christmas comes."

An Original Valentine

Tom and Sarah were the little boy and girl who lived in the small brown house near the home of Johnnie Jones. It was the evening before St. Valentine's day and the brother and sister were sitting by the fire, talking together.

"I do wish we had some valentines to send," said Tom. "If we only had some gilt or colored paper and some pictures, we could make them, but we haven't anything at all."

"I am sorry," their mother told them. "The children have been so kind to you this winter. You remember how they helped you with the coal? I wish we could send them each a very beautiful valentine to thank them, but I am afraid I can't spare the money to buy even one."

Sarah had been as quiet as a little mouse while Tom and Mother were speaking. Then suddenly she said: "I know what we can do!"

"What?" asked Tom.

Sarah began to dance about the room. "It will be such fun!" she said.

"Please tell me," begged Tom.

"Don't you see," Sarah explained; "we can't buy valentines, and we can't make valentines, so we shall just have to be valentines!"

"Now how in the world can we be valentines?" Tom asked her.

"We'll dress in our Sunday clothes," she answered. "We'll cut hearts out of paper and pin them all over us. Then we'll ask Mother to pin a paper envelope on each of us, and address it to one of the children. When we are ready we'll ring the door bell of that child's house, and when he opens the door, we'll speak mottoes, and all sorts of rhymes. Won't the children laugh?"

"All right!" said Tom. "Only, I would rather not be a valentine myself. You be one and I will send you. We'll pretend you are the doll valentine we saw down town the other day, the one that danced when the man wound her up, and spoke the verse."

"Well!" Sarah assented, "and you must wind me up and I'll dance little Sally Waters."

They spent the rest of the evening thinking of rhymes. Their mother taught them all she could remember, and Sarah repeated them over and over again so that she should not forget.

The next morning they went to school, but as soon as they had reached home and eaten their lunch they began their preparations. No one in the whole world ever saw a sweeter valentine than Sarah, when she was ready in her bright red dress and short snow-white coat, decorated with paper hearts. Then her mother cut and folded some wrapping paper into a big envelope, and placed it about Sarah's little body. Of course her feet had to be left free so that she could walk, and her head, so that she could breathe.

"Let's go to Johnnie Jones's house first," Tom said.

So his mother addressed the envelope to Master Johnnie Jones, and the children started off.

Johnnie Jones was at home that afternoon, feeling very sad. He had fallen into the pond several days before, and the icy bath had given him such a cold that he had to stay indoors. He could see the other children running about from house to house sending their valentines, and he wanted to run about and send some too. To be sure he had received ever so many, but he was tired of looking at them and hearing the mottoes read, and he wished very much that some one would come in to play with him.

Mother had just said: "I am afraid no one will come to-day, dear, because all the children are busy with their valentines," when the door bell rang.

As soon as Maggie had opened the door she called up to Johnnie Jones: "There's a beautiful valentine down here for you. I'll bring it up. Tom sent it. I caught him at the door, so I'll bring him up, too."

Johnnie Jones ran to the head of the staircase as fast as he could run. How he did laugh when Maggie placed Sarah before him, and showed him the address on the envelope.

"It's a doll valentine," Tom explained, "and it has a phonograph in it. I'll wind it up."

He knelt down and pretended to turn a crank. Then Sarah, who had not smiled or spoken a word before, said:

"If you love me as I love you, No knife can cut our love in two."

Tom turned the crank again, and this time she danced.

"Let me wind it," begged Johnnie Jones, who was very much pleased. He did, and the valentine said:

"Roses red and violets blue,   Sugar is sweet and so are you."

Mother joined the children in the hall, and was delighted with the valentine, which each one wound up until it had said all the rhymes that Sarah knew, and had danced until she was tired. Then the doll changed into a little girl for a while, and she had some milk and cookies with the other children.

"We shall have to go now," Tom said at last, looking out of the window. "The other children have gone into their houses and I must send them each a valentine."

So Mother made a new envelope and addressed it to Miss Elizabeth Elkins.

"Thank you for my valentine," said Johnnie Jones. "It's the loveliest one I have had all day, only I wish I could keep it as I can the others."

All the children who received the little Valentine in turn, made exactly the same remark, so Tom and Sarah were very happy over the success of their plan.

When Johnnie Jones was a Cry-Baby

All his life Johnnie Jones had been a bright, happy little fellow who seldom cried even when he was hurt. Therefore, everyone who knew him was surprised when suddenly, just before he was five years old, he became a cry-baby.

The trouble began with some of the older boys in the neighborhood. There were three of them who were several years older than Johnnie Jones, and a year older than the other children. Lately these big boys had commenced to tease the smaller ones, and especially Johnnie Jones. They did not intend to be unkind, but would often make him cry by rolling him off his sled, pelting him with snowballs, or calling him nicknames.

Of course, there was no reason for crying, since, although the boys were rather rough, they never really hurt Johnnie Jones. Indeed, they loved him, and were only in fun when they teased him. If Johnnie Jones had been brave enough to laugh at them he would soon have been left in peace; but as he always cried instead, the boys began to call him "crybaby."

Johnnie Jones soon formed the bad habit of crying about every little thing that did not please him, until at last it was difficult to live with him. His father and mother were greatly distressed, and tried in every way to help Johnnie Jones. They told him that they were ashamed to have a cry-baby for a son, but that only made him cry more than ever.

Finally Mother said that something must be done, for Johnnie Jones had reached the point where he was almost always crying. He would come home crying from kindergarten, he would come in from play with tears in his eyes, and worst of all, every few minutes, he would find some excuse for crying at home.

"I think he must be ill," Mother said to Father, one day, "and I am so worried that I shall take him to the doctor."

Father agreed, so in the afternoon, Mother and Johnnie Jones paid Dr. Smith a visit in his office.

Dr. Smith was a great friend of Johnnie Jones's and was sorry to hear of the crying spells. He examined the little boy very carefully, but could find nothing wrong with him. Then he said that he was sure Johnnie Jones was not ill, and that he cried so often just because he had formed a bad habit.

"It is a very disagreeable habit," he continued, "and I know you want to overcome it, so I'll write you a prescription for some medicine. Doctors usually do not prescribe for people unless they are ill, but I think if you take a spoonful of this medicine every time you cry, you will soon be cured of the habit. You try it, anyway."

He gave the prescription to Mother, who, after thanking him, left the office with Johnnie Jones. On the way home they stopped at the drug-store and bought the medicine, which mother took into the house with her, while Johnnie Jones ran out to play.

There wasn't a child in that neighborhood who was not fond of Johnnie Jones, but since he had become a cry-baby none of them cared to play with him, because he would often spoil the best game by stopping to cry. No one enjoys playing with a tearful boy or girl.

All the children were playing in the snow when Johnnie Jones joined them. They had built a snow fort, which half of the children were trying to destroy with snowballs, and which half were defending. They were having the merriest sort of a time. Occasionally some one would be struck by a ball, but he would just laugh and send back another, for it was all in fun.

Johnnie Jones began to play, too, and was enjoying himself very much, when unfortunately a stray ball struck his cheek. It did hurt, but not nearly enough to cry about, for all the balls were soft. Johnnie Jones, however, began to cry, called the children "unkind," which was foolish, and ran away home.

As soon as he entered the house, Mother gave him some of the medicine. Never was anyone more surprised than Johnnie Jones, when he tasted it! The only other medicine he had ever taken had been sweet, but this was dreadfully bitter. He had no sooner swallowed it than he began to cry again. Mother immediately poured more of it from the bottle.

"I won't take any more," Johnnie Jones, said between his sobs, "it is bad medicine."

"Yes, indeed," Mother told him, "you must take it every time you cry, just as the doctor said, because we can't continue to have a cry-baby in the house. You must take another dose now unless you can stop crying without it."

"I'll stop," said Johnnie Jones, and he did.

Mother poured some of the medicine into another bottle to send to Miss Page at kindergarten, and then placed the rest on the mantel where Johnnie Jones could see it.

It was remarkable how quickly the little boy was cured of his bad habit. After he had taken but three doses of the bitter medicine he learned to stop and think when anything failed to please him. Then, instead of allowing himself to cry, he would often manage to laugh, which was much more sensible, and much pleasanter for the people near him. Soon he began to realize what a foolish little boy he had been, and at last he made up his mind to be, instead of a cry-baby, a big, brave boy. And that is what he was, all the rest of his life, bright and sweet and brave, so that everyone loved to be with him, grown folks as well as the children.

Johnnie Jones and the Man Who Cried "Wolf" too Often

Some time passed by before people began to realize that Johnnie Jones was no longer a cry-baby. On that account he had a very unpleasant experience one day.

The children were playing horse on the sidewalk, and Johnnie Jones as one of the horses, was being driven by Sammy Smith. All went well until they reached a rough place in the pavement. Here Johnnie Jones tripped and fell, scraping his leg against a sharp stone, and straining and bruising his arm quite badly. It happened so quickly that none of the children saw that he was hurt, and so did not pity him when he began to cry. They were so accustomed to hear him cry over every little trouble, that they thought nothing of his crying then. If they had known he was really hurt, they would have been kind and helped him up. As it was, they merely told him not to be such a cry-baby and ran off and left him.

Just then Father came by on his way home, and when he saw Johnnie Jones leaning against the fence, crying, he thought, too, that the little boy had become a cry-baby again. If he had seen Johnnie Jones fall, he would have picked him up and carried him home in his arms; but not knowing that the little boy was really hurt, he took hold of his hand, and walked home with him. Johnnie Jones was trying his best not to cry, but I think the bravest boy in the world might not have been able to keep back the tears, with such a sore leg and arm.

As they entered the house, Mother said: "Oh little son! crying again?"

When she had heard of the accident, she told Johnnie Jones that she was sorry, and would try to help him after lunch. But as soon as she saw that he could eat nothing at all, she asked Father to carry him upstairs, where she examined the injured leg and arm. When she found them so badly scraped and bruised, she was greatly distressed.

"You poor little boy!" she exclaimed, "No one realized that you were really in pain."

After she had bathed and bandaged the leg and arm, and made Johnnie Jones comfortable, she brought his lunch up to him, and while he was eating, told him this story:

Once, a long, long time ago, there lived a man whose name has been forgotten. He lived with other men and their families out in the pasture lands, and there he tended the sheep. Now a great many wolves lived near by, which often tried to steal into the fold and carry off the sheep. Everyone kept a close watch for these wolves, and when any person saw one he would cry out, "wolf! wolf!" so that all the others might come to help him destroy it, and save the sheep. But this first man of whom I told you, liked to call "wolf!" when there was no wolf there, just to frighten or disturb the others. Sometimes he would waken the men at night by his foolish cry, and they would come running out only to find he had given a false alarm. At last these men grew weary of answering his calls. Besides, as there had been no wolves about for some little time, they were feeling quite safe.

One night, when the foolish man was keeping watch over his sheep, he saw in the distance an entire pack of wolves coming steadily toward the fold. Instantly he raised a loud cry, "WOLF! WOLF!" and waited for help.

But no help came.

The men heard his cry. but as they did not believe the wolves were really there, they remained in their beds. One man alone could not defend himself and his sheep against a pack of hungry wolves. So, next morning, he was found badly injured, and the sheep were gone. Everyone was sorry for the man, but all knew he could blame only himself. He had cried "wolf!" too often, when there was no wolf there, and so he was not believed when the wolf came at last.

"Johnnie Jones," said Mother, when she had finished the story, "you have cried so often when there was no reason for crying, that this one time when you cried because you were really hurt, no one believed you. I am very sorry for you, little son, but don't you see that it was no one's fault but your own?"

Johnnie Jones's Birthday Party

A few days before Johnnie Jones's fifth birthday, Mother asked him what he would like to have for a birthday present.

"A party," he answered immediately, "and I want to invite all the children who live on this street."

"Very well," Mother said, "we'll write the invitations now, on your own note paper."

Johnnie Jones gave her a joyful hug, and ran to his desk for the paper. Mother wrote upon every sheet: "Johnnie Jones will be very glad to have you come to his birthday party, Saturday afternoon, from three until five o'clock." She addressed an envelope to each one of his playmates, and Johnnie Jones stamped, sealed and mailed the invitations as soon as they were written.

Next day the postman brought the answers. The children accepted with a great deal of pleasure.

Wednesday, Thursday, and Friday seemed very long days to impatient Johnnie Jones.

"I sometimes think," he said to Mother, "that Saturday isn't coming this week."

But, when he awoke one morning, Saturday had come at last, and the party was to be that very day.

While Mother was helping him to dress in his party clothes, she said: "Remember to make everyone glad that he came to your party, and to play whatever the children wish, even if they do not choose your favorite games."

He promised to remember, and as soon as he was dressed, ran to the window to watch for his guests. He did not have long to wait before they began to arrive.

As soon as the children had removed their hats and coats, Johnnie Jones led them to a long kindergarten table, which Mother had borrowed. Each child sat down in a small red chair, and made a necklace of colored beads, which was soon finished and tied about his neck.

When all the children had arrived and all the necklaces were finished, the boys and girls gathered in the long hall, where Johnnie Jones's roller coaster was ready for them. Each child had three rides, and enjoyed them all, for the hall was unusually long, and with a good start, one could go to the end of it, almost as fast as the lightning flashes.

Of course, Johnnie Jones had his three rides after the others, because he was the host, and the children his guests.

"Now we may go to the parlor for our games," he said as he led the children down the front stairway.

The parlor was large, so there was room enough for the children to run freely about. They played "Drop the Handkerchief," and "Blind-Man's Buff," and "Going to Jerusalem," until they were tired and ready for a more quiet game. Johnnie Jones let the others choose the games, and he watched that every child had a chance to play.

After the children had rested a moment, Mother invited them to march upstairs again, for the "real" party. Johnnie Jones's auntie played the piano for them, and the children formed in line and marched to the room in which they had made the necklaces.

The same kindergarten table was there, and in the same place, but no one would ever have known it, for it had been covered with a white table cloth, and on it were vases of lovely pink roses, and dishes full of pink and white peppermint candy. Exactly in the centre was a large birthday cake with five pink candles, and every one of them lighted. At each place was a dish of ice cream in the form of a pink and white flower, though no flower ever had so sweet a taste.

At each place there was something else. There was a tiny automobile delivery wagon, with a queer little doll chauffeur, and inside it were bundles of candy. These were to be taken home, Mother said, and no one was to open the bundles at the party. Of course no one did. Besides all of these things, there were two paper bon-bons for each child, one to open at the party, and one to take home.

The children were hungry after their games, and for a while they were very quiet. When they had finished their ice cream, however, and had eaten a piece of the birthday cake, with good wishes for Johnnie Jones, they began to pull the bon-bons apart. Then there was noise enough, for the bon-bons cracked and popped, and that made the children laugh.

All, that is, except one small girl who was afraid. She was sitting next to Johnnie Jones, and she asked him to open his bon-bon without pulling it apart. Johnnie Jones liked to hear the popping sound, and he could not help thinking that Susie was foolish to object to it, but he remembered that he must make everyone happy at his party, so he did as his little neighbor asked.

Five o'clock came all too soon, and then it was time for the children to return to their homes. When they were ready in their coats and hats, they bade Mother and Johnnie Jones good-by. "Thank you for the good time we have had," they said, as they turned their happy faces homeward, wearing the necklaces and carrying the bon-bons and automobiles.

When everyone had gone, Mother held tired, happy little Johnnie Jones on her lap.

"Did you enjoy your party?" she asked him.

"Yes, Mother dear," he answered. "I had a good time, and all the children had a good time, and it was a beautiful party."

"It was a beautiful party," Mother agreed, "and I'll tell you why. It was because both you and I did all in our power to make our company happy. I am very glad," she added, "that Johnnie Jones is my little boy and that he has enjoyed his birthday."

The Sleeping Beauty

In the early spring Mother would always tell this story to Johnnie Jones.

Once upon a time there lived the most beautiful princess in the whole world. She was so sweet that everyone loved her,--all the grown people, all the children, and even all the animals. She wore such lovely dresses that everyone who was permitted to see their beauty was filled with joy, and she had a new one every day.

She lived in the most beautiful home in the whole world. The ceiling was made of blue sky, the carpet of soft green grass, and the walls were formed by lofty trees with their branches interlaced. Everywhere were flowers of different colors, red and yellow and purple. I can't tell you how lovely it was, or how happy the king, the queen and the beautiful princess were who lived there.

One day the princess decided to make for herself a dress as white as snow, trimmed with shining pearls and sparkling diamonds. If the queen had known her intention, she would have forbidden the princess to touch a needle. I will tell you why.

When the princess was a tiny baby, the king and queen had forgotten to ask one old fairy lady to the christening. As it happened, she wasn't a good old fairy lady. Perhaps that is why she was forgotten. She came to the christening without an invitation, which was very rude, and made herself most disagreeable while she was there. She told the king and queen that because they had forgotten her, the princess should one day prick herself with a needle and immediately go to sleep, and that she should never awake unless the splendid prince should chance to find her.

Now the princess did not know of this, and she forgot to tell her mother that she intended to make the dress. That was the cause of all the trouble.

The princess cut and sewed, and sewed and cut, until the dress was finished. Then she laid aside her old gown, of red and brown, and dressed herself in the new one. She was just about to replace the needle in the workbasket, before showing herself to her mother, when, suddenly, she pricked her finger.

Immediately she sank back on her bed fast asleep. At that very instant the king and queen fell asleep, too. So did the animals, but the birds flew away. Even the little flies, who had been buzzing on the walls, went fast asleep. Then it was very still everywhere, because no one was stirring to make a noise. Even the trees were quiet, for their leaves had all dropped off, and they seemed to be sleeping too.

They slept a long, long time.

Then, the most splendid prince in all the world approached the palace gate. This prince had wonderful golden hair, and he was clothed entirely in shining gold. He rode in a chariot so bright that it could be seen for many miles. His horses were swift and he travelled fast, on his journey throughout the world.

When at last he reached the princess's house, he regarded it with wonder.

"How very quiet," he murmured. "Can it be that anyone lives in this gloomy place?"

He stepped out of his chariot and tiptoed in, through the open door. He stepped so softly that no one could have heard him, but he shone so brightly that he made the whole house light.

The splendid prince saw that everybody and everything was fast asleep.

In their rooms he found the king and queen.

At last he came to the room where lying upon her bed was the princess.

Very lovely she was, in her dress as white as snow trimmed with pearls and diamonds. The prince leaned over to see her better, and he made the diamonds sparkle so brilliantly that if you had been there you would have needed to close your eyes.

"This is the most beautiful princess in all the world," said the prince. "I wish she would waken."

Then he kissed her.

Immediately the beautiful princess opened her eyes and looked at the prince. At that same moment the king and queen awoke from their sleep. So did the animals, and all the flowers, and the little buds on the trees. The flies began to buzz about on the walls, and the birds came flying back, singing their sweetest songs.

The princess was very happy to be awake again. She attired herself in a lovely dress, indeed the loveliest one that she possessed. It was bright green, with jewels as clear as the rain drops. Then the king and queen ordered a marriage feast, and the beautiful princess married the splendid prince.

Johnnie Jones and the Butterfly

"Be careful! Don't step on that caterpillar," said Mother.

"Why not?" asked Johnnie Jones. "It's such an ugly caterpillar."

"It can't help being ugly," Mother answered, "and besides some day it will be a beautiful butterfly."

"Really?" Johnnie Jones asked, much surprised. Then Mother told him a story about a caterpillar and a butterfly.

Once upon a time, a little caterpillar was crawling slowly up a tree. "Oh! dear," he said to himself, "I wish I had wings like the birds, and could fly away to the top of a tree, instead of having to crawl slowly about."

A beautiful butterfly was resting a moment near by and heard what the little caterpillar said, "How would you like to be a beautiful butterfly such as I am," she asked him, "and go flying about all day, sipping honey from the flowers?"

"I should like it very much indeed," he answered, "but you see I am only an ugly little caterpillar who can do nothing but crawl, and I have to be very careful to avoid being stepped upon."

"I'll tell you a lovely secret,"
Whispered the butterfly.
"Next summer you will surely be
As beautiful as I,
  "Because my gauzy wings you see,
Are very, very new.
A caterpillar once was I
And crawled about like you."

The ugly little caterpillar did not believe the beautiful butterfly. He just laughed.

"Oh!" said the lovely butterfly,
"All that I say is true.
But you can't stay there very long,
There's work for you to do.
  "To the very top of this big tree
You must begin to go,
Because all little crawling things,
They are so very slow.
  "There you must even change your skin
Till it becomes dark brown.
And you must spin a rope of silk
To tie you tightly down.
  "You will sleep through the long cold winter,
When the icy winds do blow.
You will sleep through the long cold winter,
When everywhere there's snow.

"But by and by, in the spring-time,
How happy you will be!
For you will wake and find yourself
A butterfly like me!
　"Then work on, crawling little thing,"
Whispered the butterfly,
"For winter's coming very fast,
And so good-by, good-by."

The little caterpillar thought: "How could I possibly turn into a butterfly? I have seen other caterpillars tie themselves to twigs, but they always seemed very foolish to me."

However, that little caterpillar wanted more than anything else in the world to become a butterfly, so he decided to try. He crawled slowly up the tree until he found a branch that suited him exactly. Then he selected a twig and spun about it a soft resting place of silk. He spun a soft silken loop, too, with which he tied himself to the twig.

Very soon he lost all his bright color, and became as brown as the twig itself. If you had seen him, you would probably have thought he was nothing but a small brown leaf. When the cold, snowy days came, the little caterpillar knew nothing whatever about them, for he was fast asleep.

At last, after a long, long winter, there began to be signs of spring. Soon, soft warm little rain drops began to fall on the chrysalis (for that is what we call the sleeping caterpillar), whispering: "Spring is coming and it's time to awake!" Soon, soft warm little sunbeams began to dance on the chrysalis, whispering: "Spring is almost here, it is time to awake!" Soon soft, warm little breezes began to blow the chrysalis about, whispering: "Spring is here, and it is time to awake!"

Then, at last, the little caterpillar did awake. He slowly broke away his old dried skin and the silk fastenings which he had spun so many months before, and he crawled out in the sunshine, wet and still drowsy after his long sleep. After a while he became warm and dry, and wide awake in the bright sunlight, and then, suddenly, he felt that he had wings! He looked in a rain-drop mirror, and there he saw himself a beautiful butterfly.

Don't you think he must have been very proud and happy, as he spread his wings and flew away to sip the honey from the flowers, and to play with all the other butterflies, knowing that he would never again have to crawl about on the ground?

"Oh! Mother dear," said Johnnie Jones, "let's take this caterpillar home, so I can watch it turn into a butterfly."

Mother considered his idea a good one, so they carried the caterpillar home on a twig, with many leaves from the tree towards which it had been crawling. When they reached the house they placed twigs, leaves and caterpillar in a glass jar, with netting over the top.

"We shall have to give it fresh leaves every day," Mother said, "until it has eaten enough and goes to sleep. We can watch it carefully through this glass jar."

Johnnie Jones knelt down beside the jar and whispered: "Ugly little caterpillar, if you will tie yourself to that branch, and change your skin, and go to sleep, next spring you will wake a beautiful butterfly."

Johnnie Jones was sure the caterpillar heard what he said, because it went to sleep just as it was told. All winter long the little boy watched it, and one day, in the early spring, really saw it come out a gorgeous butterfly. When it spread its bright wings and flew away, I wonder which was happier, the butterfly or Johnnie Jones.

Mr. and Mrs. Bird and the Baby Birds

"Listen to that bird!" exclaimed Johnnie Jones.

"That is Mr. Bird," Mother answered. "I shall have to tell you a story about him and Mrs. Bird and their children."

Once upon a time Mr. Bird felt so happy and gay that he could scarcely be quiet a single moment. It was spring-time again and he sang beautiful songs to Mrs. Bird, about the sunshine and soft, sweet air, and about the little home they would make in the old elm tree. Mrs. Bird would listen for a while to his song and then they would both fly away to find the twigs and straws with which to build the nest. Very hard indeed the little birds worked, for each straw had to be carefully woven, in and out and out and in, so that the nest should be quite firm and round.

As soon as the nest was ready, pretty little Mrs. Bird laid four lovely blue eggs in it. She knew, and Mr. Bird knew, that there were four baby birds asleep in the eggs, and so they were happier than ever before.

But now Mrs. Bird had to sit on the nest all the day long, to keep the eggs warm. Of course, Mr. Bird had to feed her. He would fly all over the park, finding good things to eat, and carry them back to drop into Mrs. Bird's mouth. When she was no longer hungry, Mr. Bird would hop to a branch near by, and sing to her.

You may think that Mrs. Bird grew tired of sitting there on the nest day after day. You may think Mr. Bird became tired of feeding Mrs. Bird, and of singing to her, day after day. But neither one seemed to grow tired at all. They just watched and waited, as the days went by.

After a while the little baby birds began to wake up, and one day Mrs. Bird heard a queer scratching sound that made her very glad. The babies were beginning to break open the shell! Peck! Peck! Peck! Soon a little head came out of the shell. Crack! Crack! Crack! and there was a little bird in the nest for Mr. and Mrs. Bird to love and take care of.

By the time the first pieces of shell had been thrown from the nest, another little bird had broken through. Then came another, and still one more, until there were four baby birds in the nest, all crying as loud as they could, "Peep! Peep! Peep! please give us something to eat."

Then both Mr. and Mrs. Bird had to fly away to seek their own breakfast, and to bring some to the children. You never saw such hungry babies! They kept their parents busy all the day long, bringing them food. They weren't very polite to each other, either, those baby birds. They would crowd and push, and almost send each other out of the nest, trying to get every morsel, instead of each waiting his own turn to be fed. But then, they were only birds and did not know any better.

Day after day, they were fed by their parents. Night after night, they were kept warm under Mrs. Bird's wings. No wonder those baby birds soon grew big and strong. They were ever so much prettier when they grew big enough to wear feathers.

Soon, one little bird felt so strong, that he said he wanted to fly away, too, and see what the ground and other trees were like.

"Not to-day," Mrs. Bird told him. "Wait until your wings are a wee bit stronger, and then I'll teach you to fly."

When both Mr. and Mrs. Bird had flown away, this same little bird said to his brothers: "It seems quite easy to fly; all you need to do is to flap your wings. I think I'll try it alone."

"You had better not!" the others told him.

"Yes, I will," the little bird said.

He hopped to the edge of the nest, and began to flap his wings. He did not quite dare to raise his feet, though, for he felt rather timid when he looked down and saw how far away the ground seemed to be. But he flapped his wings so vigorously, pretending to fly, that he lost his balance and fell. He was not hurt, for the grass was tall and soft, but he was greatly frightened, and cried out for his mother.

Mrs. Bird was too far away to hear him, but a little girl did. She picked him up very gently, and ran to show him to her father.

"Look at this cunning little bird which I have found! May I keep it for mine?" she asked him.

"No," said her father. "See, it is only a baby bird, which has fallen from its nest, and is crying for its mother. Show me where you found it; perhaps I can reach the nest if we can discover it among the leaves."

The little girl pointed out the tree to her father. He placed a ladder against it, and, climbing up, was able to drop the little bird into its home.

In a few days Mr. and Mrs. Bird were ready to teach all their babies to fly.

"Come on," they said, "spread your wings, jump into the air, and fly just a little way, to that other limb of the tree."

Three of the little birds obeyed at once, and reached the resting place in safety. But the fourth little bird was afraid to try, because he had fallen before.

"Don't be a coward," urged his father and mother. "You fell before because your wings were not strong enough to bear you up, but now you will have no trouble."

The little bird wouldn't budge.

The parent birds knew it was time for him to learn, so they pushed the foolish little fellow out of the nest, and watched him spread his wings, and flutter to the ground. There he found more courage, and after a while he flew up to join his brothers on the tree.

"I was sitting at my window," Mother told Johnnie Jones, "and saw it all happen. Of course I can't understand the language of birds, and I am not sure I have repeated exactly what the parent birds said to the babies, or what the babies said to each other, but only what they seemed to say. Anyway, everything happened as I have told you."

"Soon the babies could fly nearly as well and as far as the old birds, and after that the little nest was left quite empty, rocked by the wind in the old tree top."

The Coming of Little Brother

Almost all of the children who attended the kindergarten where Johnnie Jones spent his mornings, had a baby brother or sister at home. They spoke of "their babies" so often and enjoyed so much making presents to take them, that Johnnie Jones wished for a baby at his house, and talked to Mother about it.

One night, Mother said she had a secret to tell him. He was glad, for he liked to have secrets with Mother, who told him a great many, because he could keep them so well.

"It is the most beautiful secret in all the world," Mother said. "Spring-time is coming very fast, and next month, when the trees and the flowers wake up because winter is over and gone, a dear little baby is coming to live with us."

"Oh! Mother dear, I am so glad!" said Johnnie Jones. "But why does the baby wait so long? I want him this very day."

"Dear," Mother answered, "the baby is still fast asleep, just as the little flower buds are, and we must watch and wait until he comes. It will not be very long, little son, and then how happy we'll be, you and Father and I!"

"At first the baby will be too small and helpless to play, and will need his big brother to take care of him so that he may grow tall and strong. Then, by and by, he will be able to run about and talk, and play with you. But always, always, he will need you to help him, and teach him, and care for him."

After that evening, when Mother had whispered the beautiful secret to him, Johnnie Jones would ask her each day: "Will our baby wake up and come tomorrow?" But Mother could not tell him, so they just waited, and made ready, day after day.

At last one bright, warm morning when Johnnie Jones awoke, he saw Father bending down over his bed with such a happy face that he asked at once: "Has our baby waked up and come?"

"Yes," Father answered, "there is a Little Brother in Mother's room, and she says she can't wait any longer to show him to you."

Johnnie Jones was very much excited and, as soon as possible, he tiptoed into Mother's room. Father had asked him to be very quiet.

"Come here, dear," Mother said, "I have been waiting such a long time for you." She drew him down beside her, and showed him a tiny baby boy no larger than a doll.

As Johnnie Jones leaned down to see, the Little Brother opened his eyes wide, and looked at him. Johnnie Jones was too happy to say a word. He sat down close to the bed, and Father placed the baby in his arms. Johnnie Jones held him very carefully, so that he might not hurt him or let him fall.

"He is your Little Brother," Mother said softly, "your Little Brother to love and take care of all your life. You will always remember that, won't you?"

And Johnnie Jones always did.

Little Brother and Johnnie Jones

Little brother was a merry baby with a smile for everyone. Soon he was old enough to be on the floor with Johnnie Jones, and to build houses of blocks, and play with the toys. He learned to walk very early, when he was less than a year old. Then indeed, he kept the family busy, guarding him from harm.

One day he found the sharp scissors, which Johnnie Jones had to take away very quickly before he could cut himself. Another day he tried to eat a paper of pins, and Johnnie Jones had to run very fast to reach him in time. That one baby kept Father and Mother, Johnnie Jones and Maggie, all busy, because he was too young to know that some things are dangerous for babies to have.

Sometimes, because he was too little to know any better, he objected to having the scissors, or knives, or cookies, taken away. Then what do you suppose he would do? He would run straight to Johnnie Jones and pull his hair! He always seemed to feel happier after that.

It hurts to have one's hair pulled, but Johnnie Jones seldom cried or was cross with the baby. He would just laugh and run away when he saw him coming for his hair. Besides, that bad habit did not last long, and you may be sure that Johnnie Jones was glad when it was broken!

The first word the baby learned to say after "Mama" was "Buddy," and he meant Johnnie Jones. He knew when it was time for the big boy to come home from kindergarten, and he would stand at the window watching for him. As soon as he saw him coming he would wave his hand, and run to the steps to meet him. Then they would have a romp. Their favorite game was "I Spy."

One day they were playing "I Spy," and Little Brother was hiding. Usually it was very easy to find him, because his favorite hiding place was the nearest corner. But this time he wasn't there when Johnnie Jones looked, nor anywhere in the room or hall.

"Where can he be?" Johnnie Jones asked Mother.

She came to help him. They called the baby but heard no answer. Then they began to be worried and looked in every room. Suddenly they heard a great splash in the bath-tub. They ran into the bathroom, and there they found the baby.

Little Brother had forgotten he was playing "I Spy." He had wandered into the bath-room, and climbing on a chair dropped the soap into the tub which was full of water. Then, very soon, he dropped himself in, too! That was the splash the others had heard.

Mother and Johnnie Jones lifted him out, wet as he could be, and very much frightened.

"You dear little rascal!" exclaimed Johnnie Jones. "Didn't you know you couldn't swim?"

"It certainly is a good thing," Mother said, "that he has a big brother to take care of him."

Elizabeth with the Children

One day Elizabeth came over to spend the afternoon with Johnnie Jones, who was very glad to see her.

"Let's play horse," suggested Johnnie Jones. "I have a new pair of reins with bells on them."

"No, I don't want to play horse," Elizabeth said. "I want to play "I Spy," and I want to hide. You must find me."

"All right!" answered Johnnie Jones.

But as soon as it was Johnnie Jones's turn to hide, and Elizabeth's to find him, she decided that she would rather play fire-engine. "I'll be the fireman and put out the fire with your real little hose, and you be the horse and engine," she said.

"All right," Johnnie Jones answered again.

After they had extinguished several fires, Elizabeth said: "Now we'll play grocery-store, and I'll be the man who keeps it. We'll borrow some apples and potatoes from the cook, and you come to buy them."

"No," said Johnnie Jones this time, "I'll be the grocery man, and you the lady who comes to buy."

"I won't play if I mayn't be the storekeeper," threatened Elizabeth.

"But that's not fair," said Johnnie Jones. "You have chosen every game, and have taken the best part in each one for yourself. Now it is my turn to choose."

"I'll go home if you won't let me be the grocery man," Elizabeth told him.

"No," he answered, "because that's not a fair way to play."

Then Elizabeth left him. She did not go home, however, but just next door to Katherine's house. She found Katherine and Mary at home, playing with their dolls.

As soon as the little girls saw Elizabeth, they said: "You can't play with us unless you play the right way. You can't be Mother all the time."

"Well, if you won't let me play my way, I won't play at all," said Elizabeth, and ran on until she came to Sarah's house.

Sarah, Tom and Ned were jumping rope, and they called out to Elizabeth: "You can't play with us unless you will turn the rope part of the time."

"I don't like to turn, I like to jump," Elizabeth complained. But when she realized that she would not be allowed to jump until she first turned the rope for the others, she left these children too, and went next door to visit Sammy Smith.

That little boy and Susie were playing with a big wagon. They asked Elizabeth to play with them, and because they were courteous little children, and she was their visitor, they permitted her to take the first ride, and pretended that they were two strong horses hitched to her carriage. When they were tired, they told Elizabeth that it was time for her to become a horse and let one of them ride.

"No," said Elizabeth, "I like to ride better than to pull the wagon."

"We won't let you ride any longer," they answered, "because it's your turn to play that you are a horse."

"Then I'll go home," she said, and this time she did.

"What is the matter?" asked her mother.

"The children won't play the way I want them to, and I don't like them any more because I think they are unkind," she answered. "I wish I could go to fairy-land and be a princess, or else that I were a grown-up lady."

"Even grown-up ladies and princesses cannot always have their own way," her mother said.

Elizabeth stood at the window and looked out across the street. Most of the children had gathered there in front of Johnnie Jones's house, and were jumping rope. Elizabeth could hear them counting, and laughing, and talking. She began to feel very lonely. At last she put on her hat again and ran back to join the children.

"If you will let me play with you," she said, "I'll play anything you like."

"All right!" they answered, "and sometimes we'll play what you like."

"And I won't always ask for the best part any more," she said.

"You may have the part you like when it is your turn to choose," they told her.

"I'll turn the rope now," Elizabeth added.

"You turn until some one trips," the others answered.

Elizabeth spent the remainder of the afternoon with the children, who were glad to have her because she played fair. Elizabeth herself was very happy. She was even glad that she wasn't a princess or a grown-up lady; glad that she was just a little girl who had learned to play with other children.

Johnnie Jones and the Hoop-Rolling Club

One day, all the children of the neighborhood decided to form a hoop-rolling club. Each child was to buy a hoop and decorate it with bells and ribbons. Then, every Saturday morning, all of them were to go to the park and have a procession. They were to try their best to turn square corners, to roll their hoops in a straight line, and to keep them from falling down. No matter where they rolled them, up hill or down hill, over smooth ground or rough, they were not to let the hoops fall.

The one who could do all these things the best was to be the captain and lead the procession wherever he wished. He could go swiftly or slowly, just as he liked, and all the rest were to follow in the same manner. The captain was to remain captain only so long as he could roll his hoop better than anyone else in the club.

The children were delighted with their plan, and ran to the shop to buy the hoops.

All except poor little Johnnie Jones! He was not quite as old as the others, and he could not manage a hoop. He had tried to roll one belonging to Sammy Smith, one day, but he had been unable to prevent its falling down every time he struck it. Of course he wanted to join the club, and he asked Mother what she thought he had better do.

Mother went with him to the grocery-store, and bought a small hoop, much smaller than Sammy Smith's. Then she told Johnnie Jones that no one could teach him to roll it. "You must just try and try until you succeed, little boy," she said.

Johnnie Jones tried, all the way home, but he was as unsuccessful with the new hoop as he had been with Sammy Smith's old one. The other children watched him, but they did not know how to help him, much as they wished to do so. One big boy was rude enough to laugh at him, which hurt his feelings so much that he went out into his back yard to practise. There he tried, and tried again, until he was very tired.

Every day while the other children were decorating their hoops or were playing together, Johnnie Jones would practise all alone in the back yard, where no one could see him. He tried so hard that at last he succeeded in rolling his hoop from the porch to the gate without letting it fall a single time. He was greatly encouraged then, but he had to continue practising, because he could not even yet guide the hoop very well, and he could not turn corners at all.

When Saturday came, he went to the park to watch the first procession. It was a very pretty sight, for the hoops had been decorated with bright ribbons, and with bells which made a merry tinkling sound. Ned was the captain, as he was the oldest and could manage his hoop most skilfully. He led the children through the park, stopping now and then for breath. Whenever anyone dropped his hoop, he had to go to the end of the line, for that was the rule of the club.

All the next week Johnnie Jones worked very hard, learning to guide his hoop in a straight line, and to turn corners. He went to the park to practise now, so that he might have more room.

Mother watched him every day, and after a while she told him that he had become quite skilful enough to join the club. Then he was very happy, and began to decorate his hoop with the bright pink ribbon and shining brass bells which Mother had bought for him.

The next Saturday morning, Johnnie Jones took his hoop with him when he went to the park with the other children, all of whom were glad to hear that he had learned to roll it.

"But you had better be last in the procession," they told him, "because, most likely, you can't manage it very well yet."

They did not know how hard he had worked.

When the procession started off, Johnnie Jones kept up with the other children. Not once did he let his hoop fall, and he made it go so straight, and turned such square corners, that, presently, the children noticed how well he was doing.

"Well, look at little Johnnie Jones!" they said. "He can roll his hoop better than anyone here, even better than Ned!"

After they had watched him for a while, they decided he must be their captain, until Ned, or one of the other children had learned to do better than he.

Then Johnnie Jones was the proudest, happiest little boy in the whole world, as he led the procession through the park.

The Fire at Johnnie Jones's House

One night, while Father was away from home on a business trip, Mother and Johnnie Jones and Little Brother were fast asleep in their beds. Jack had been asleep too, down-stairs in the front hall, but now he was wide awake. He stood up, put back his ears, and sniffed the air. Then he ran quickly up the stairs to Johnnie Jones's room, stood outside his door, and whined, That did not waken anyone, so he barked.

Johnnie Jones woke up and heard him. So did mother, who was in the next room. "Please lie still, Mother," said Johnnie Jones. "I'll see what is the matter." He was trying to help Mother all he could while Father was away.

He opened the door, and cried out: "Oh, Mother, the hall is full of smoke!"

Mother came to the door. She saw that smoke was pouring out from the hall below. "I am afraid the house is on fire," she said. "You must be very brave and help me. Put on your wrapper and slippers and run up to Maggie's room, and tell her and Kathie to come down here."

Johnnie Jones was a bit frightened, but without another word he ran up those long, dark steps, and aroused the two girls. It was brave of the little boy.

Meanwhile Mother had given the fire alarm through the telephone, slipped on her wrapper, and bundled the baby in a blanket. When the others had come down to her room, she closed the door into the hall.

"It would be dangerous to go downstairs," she said; "we must just wait here at the window until the firemen bring us a ladder."

"Oh, Mother!" Johnnie Jones said, "do you think they'll come soon?"

"Listen!" Mother answered.

Then Johnnie Jones heard a sound that made him clap his hands with joy. CLANG! CLANG! CLANG! Galloping down the street came the splendid big fire-horses drawing the hook-and-ladder. CLANG! CLANG! CLANG! Down the street came the fire-engine, the hose carriage, and the salvage corps wagon.

Quick as a flash the firemen saw Mother and the children at the window! Quicker than you can think, they had two long ladders placed against the two window sills. Then two strong firemen climbed up. One of them helped Mother and the baby to reach the ground, the other looked after Johnnie Jones.

Maggie and Kathie did not wait to be helped, they stepped down the ladder faster than one would have thought possible, and reached the ground first of all.

Jack did not know how to use a ladder, so he was thrown out of the window by one fireman, and caught in a blanket by two others. He wasn't hurt in the least, though Johnnie Jones had been worried for fear he might be, but ran straight to his little master.

"If it had not been for Jack's telling us there was a fire, we might not have been able to leave the house so quickly," said Mother, as she caressed the dog.

Elizabeth's mother, who lived across the street, asked Mrs. Jones and the children to come into her house. They went, and stood at the window watching the fire until it was out.

It was a beautiful sight, for the flames flashed out of the thick smoke and made the whole neighborhood bright. Poor Mother felt too sad at seeing her home burn to enjoy the beauty of the fire, but as it was the very first fire he had ever seen, Johnnie Jones did enjoy it, although he was sorry, too.

"Never mind, Mother dear," he said, trying to comfort her. "Father will build us a new house if this one burns down."

All this time the brave firemen were working to extinguish the fire. They had unhitched the horses, and tied them, at a safe distance from the house. Some of them had fixed the hose to the engine and were pumping great streams of water onto the flames. Others were inside the house fighting the fire; and the salvage men were trying to save the furniture and pictures and curtains.

Soon the flames became lower, and lower, until at last they died away, and the fire was out. Then the horses were hitched again to the engine, and hose carriage, and the other wagons. The whistle in the engine was blown, and all went back to the engine houses where they belonged. Not as they had come, in a swift gallop, but slowly, for now men and horses were tired.

Soon the neighborhood was quiet again, and everyone returned to bed. The Jones's passed the rest of the night in Elizabeth's house.

Next morning, they drove to Grandmother's home to visit her until they could go into the country to spend the summer.

When Father came home he was very much grieved to find his home so badly burned, but he felt very grateful to Jack for arousing the family, and he was very thankful to the brave firemen and good horses, for coming so quickly and doing their work so well. He was distressed that he had not been at home, to save Mother from worry and care, but he was glad to hear that Johnnie Jones had been a help and comfort to her, and had behaved as a manly boy should.

Johnnie Jones and Fanny

Johnnie Jones enjoyed the country because he could be out of doors all the day long, and because there were so many interesting things to do. This summer he liked it even better than ever before, for Little Brother was old enough to run about and play with him, in the soft grass under the trees.

Then there was Fanny.

Fanny was a small brown pony which lived in the country all the year round, and which had belonged to Johnnie Jones ever since he was a tiny boy only two years old. The little pony and the little boy loved each other, and spent a great deal of their time together. Each morning, directly after breakfast, Johnnie Jones and Little Brother would go down to the field where Fanny and the horses lived, taking with them an apple or some sugar.

"Here, Fanny! Here, Fanny!" they would call.

As soon as she heard their voices, the little brown pony would come running to them and eat out of their hands, always being very careful not to nip their fingers. Then she would poke her nose into Johnnie Jones's pockets to see if there were anything hidden away, that was good to eat. She was so sweet tempered and gentle that she would let the children do anything with her that pleased them, and often romped with Johnnie Jones like a big dog.

About nine o'clock, Sam, the hired man, would hitch Fanny to a small cart, and Johnnie Jones would take Mother, or Maggie, and Little Brother, for a drive. Johnnie Jones could both drive and ride so very well that he was often allowed to go out with Fanny quite alone.

One morning, after he had taken the others home, he started to the village shop to buy some butter. On the road he met a boy named Charley, who asked to go with him.

"All right! Jump in," Johnnie Jones told him, glad to have company.

"Let me drive?" Charley asked. So Johnnie Jones changed places with him, and gave him the reins.

Charley was older than Johnnie Jones and considered himself a much better driver, but he did not know and love horses in the same way that Johnnie Jones did, though he had always lived in the country.

"Watch me!" he said. "I'll show you how to make a pony run."

Before Johnnie Jones could stop him, he seized the whip and with it gave Fanny a sharp cut. The little pony had never before been whipped, and was so surprised and hurt, that she began to run as fast as ever she could. Bump! Bump! She dragged the cart over rocks and stones so fast that the little boys were almost thrown out on the road.

Johnnie Jones was just as surprised as Fanny.

"Give me that whip," he said to Charley. "I don't allow anyone to use it on my pony. You've hurt her and made her run away. Give me the reins. I will never again let you drive."

"Leave me alone," Charley answered. "I'll teach her a good lesson."

He struck Fanny once more, and then began pulling on the reins with all his might, hurting the pony's tender mouth, and making her toss her head and even kick.

Johnnie Jones was very angry and commanded Charley to give him the reins. Charley was beginning to be frightened, so he obeyed.

"Whoa! Fanny, don't be afraid," Johnnie Jones said to the little pony, as he took the reins and held them loosely in his hands.

As soon as Fanny heard the voice of her little master, she stopped running, and soon stood still. Then Johnnie Jones jumped out of the cart and began to pat her. Fanny was very much ashamed of herself, and rubbed her nose against his sleeve, as if to say: "I am sorry, Johnnie Jones, but that boy surprised me. I'll never act so again."

Johnnie Jones drove on to the shop and then back home, but he was so angry with Charley that he would not let him ride any further.

"I don't like you any more," he told him.

And I do not blame Johnnie Jones, do you? For I could not like a boy who would be so cowardly and unkind as to hurt an animal.

Fanny and Little Brother

One day, Elizabeth came with her mother to spend the day in the country with Mrs. Jones and the little boys. The children had enjoyed themselves very much, playing all the morning. Just before lunch they ran down to the field where Fanny and Tim, the carriage horse, were, to pick some wild flowers for the table. Little Brother was with them, and while the others were gathering the flowers, he toddled away, and lay down in the tall grass.

The two mothers were sitting under the trees near the house. From where they sat they could see the children in the field.

"Aren't you afraid to let the children play there where the horses are?" Elizabeth's mother asked Mrs. Jones.

"No indeed," she answered. "Tim and Fanny love them too well to hurt them."

But just then Tim and Fanny began to play "Tag," as they often did, for they were great friends. Fanny pretended to bite Tim, and came galloping up the field as fast as ever she could. She did not see Little Brother, lying directly in front of her, hidden by the tall grass. On she came, galloping rapidly towards him.

Mother saw her, and was so frightened she could hardly stand, for she thought the baby would be trampled down by the pony. She started to run, but of course she could not run as fast as Fanny, and besides, she was much further away.

Fanny rushed on until she was within a few feet of the baby. Then she saw him! She tried to stop, but was moving too rapidly. Being a wise little pony, she saw there was but one thing to do, and she did it. She jumped and landed on the other side of the baby without touching him, though her foot just did miss his head.

Mother caught Little Brother up in her arms, and examined him carefully. She could scarcely believe he had escaped without any injury, and was very happy indeed, when she found that such was the case.

"I don't believe any other pony would have had so much sense," she said.

That evening, when Father had heard of Little Brother's narrow escape, he told Mother and Johnnie Jones about an experience he had had when a baby.

His father had owned a wise old horse whose name was Charley. One day Charley was eating the grass in the yard, and Johnnie Jones's father, who was then only a baby three years old, was lying on the ground, playing with the leaves After a while old Charley had eaten all the grass near by, except the very long delicious blades underneath the baby. He couldn't ask the little boy to move away, because he couldn't talk. So, very carefully, he took hold of the baby's dress with his teeth, lifted him up, and set him down on the other side of the yard. He did not even frighten him, but the mother, who was looking out of the window, was very much frightened, until she saw that the baby had not been harmed.

Mother and Johnnie Jones agreed that Charley had shown almost as much sense as Fanny, but that it wasn't very safe to leave little children alone when there were horses and ponies about.

When Johnnie Jones Learned to Swim

One summer, when Johnnie Jones was six, he and the other members of the family spent a month in the woods. They lived in a small log house which was close to a beautiful lake, and almost completely surrounded by trees. Johnnie Jones enjoyed the life there immensely. He learned to row a light boat on the water, and every day he went for a long walk through the woods, meeting many birds and small wild animals on the way. Sometimes, in the distance, he caught a glimpse of the beautiful, graceful deer, which were too timid to permit him to come very near them.

Just in front of the house was a wooden dock where Johnnie Jones liked to play, but where he was never allowed to go alone as the water about it was very deep. "Teach me to swim," he said to his father. "Then I shall be able to play wherever I please."

Father had been intending to give Johnnie Jones lessons in swimming and was only waiting for a warm, sunshiny day. Such a day came very soon, and, about twelve o'clock, he and Johnnie Jones, dressed in their bathing suits, went in the water. The little boy considered bathing great fun as long as he remained close to shore where the water was shallow but he did not like it so well when Father carried him out to the raft, where the water was so deep that it reached the shoulders of the grown people standing in it.

"Now, son," Mr. Jones said, "I want you to stand on the raft, and jump when I count three. I will catch you in my arms, let you go down under the water, and bring you up again. Remember to hold your breath, so that you will not take any of the water into your nose or mouth. Perhaps you had better keep one hand over your face for fear you might forget and try to breathe before you reach the surface. Now jump, I am quite ready to catch you."

Johnnie Jones stood on the raft and looked down at the water. He did not want to jump into it, but neither did he want to disappoint his father. Besides he wished very much to learn to swim.

"Will you be certain to catch me?" he asked Father.

"I promise you I will," he answered.

Johnnie Jones knew that Father always kept his promise, so, after a moment or two, he said he was ready.

"One, two, three, jump!" said Father. And Johnnie Jones obeyed.

As soon as he touched the water he felt Father's strong arms about him, and then he did not mind going down, down, into it. In a second he came to the surface again, of course dripping wet, but without having swallowed any water, as he had remembered to hold his breath.

After the first plunge, he enjoyed taking others, and jumped into the water as many times as Father would catch him. Next day they went in bathing again, and Father carried Johnnie Jones out to the raft as before. But when the little boy was ready to jump, Father said: "To-day, I shall not catch you when you first touch the water; I shall wait until you come to the surface by yourself, and then I shall hold you up."

After he had jumped into the water, Johnnie Jones was surprised to find that he came up again just as quickly as when Father's arms had been under him. Then while Father held him he lay flat on the water and paddled himself about with his hands and feet.

In a few days the little boy learned to swim a short distance, quite alone, although he was not allowed to go into the water unless an older person were with him.

One day, before Johnnie Jones had learned to swim very well, he had an exciting experience. He was on the dock with his uncle, and a very high wind was blowing the water into waves, which dashed against the dock with a roaring sound. Indeed the waves were so noisy, that when Johnnie Jones suddenly slipped and fell off the dock, his uncle, whose back was turned, did not hear the splash.

However, a boatman at the boat-house saw Johnnie Jones fall, and he ran as fast as possible, towards the dock.

Meantime Johnnie Jones sank down into the water, and came up to the surface again. The brave little fellow remembered what to do. He closed his mouth, and holding one hand over his nose, he paddled with the other, until he was able to grasp the dock, against which the wind was blowing him. He held on bravely, never opening his mouth to cry, nor taking his hand from his face.

In less than a minute, though it seemed much longer to Johnnie Jones, his uncle and the boatman had drawn him from the water. He was not in the least harmed by his unexpected bath because he had remembered, even while he was falling, the proper thing to do.

Mother stripped off his wet clothing, and after she had rubbed him until he was all in a glow, she wrapped him in blankets so that he should not take cold.

Johnnie Jones went to sleep. When he awoke he felt very well, and was glad when he heard Father say: "You were a brave boy and I am proud of you."

Johnnie Jones's uncle was sorry he had been so careless as to turn his back when the wind was blowing such a gale, and promised that it should never happen again.

Johnnie Jones was more careful, too, and had no further trouble in the water. Every day, Father gave him a swimming lesson, and before the time came to return to the city, Johnnie Jones felt very much at home in the water. He could swim very well, and could float, lying flat on his back, but another summer passed before he had quite learned to dive.

The Codes Of Hammurabi And Moses
W. W. Davies

QTY

The discovery of the Hammurabi Code is one of the greatest achievements of archaeology, and is of paramount interest, not only to the student of the Bible, but also to all those interested in ancient history...

Religion   **ISBN:** *1-59462-338-4*   **Pages:132**
MSRP $12.95

The Theory of Moral Sentiments
Adam Smith

QTY

This work from 1749. contains original theories of conscience amd moral judgment and it is the foundation for systemof morals.

Philosophy ISBN: *1-59462-777-0*   **Pages:536**
MSRP $19.95

Jessica's First Prayer
Hesba Stretton

QTY

In a screened and secluded corner of one of the many railway-bridges which span the streets of London there could be seen a few years ago, from five o'clock every morning until half past eight, a tidily set-out coffee-stall, consisting of a trestle and board, upon which stood two large tin cans, with a small fire of charcoal burning under each so as to keep the coffee boiling during the early hours of the morning when the work-people were thronging into the city on their way to their daily toil...

Childrens   ISBN: *1-59462-373-2*   **Pages:84**
MSRP $9.95

My Life and Work
Henry Ford

QTY

Henry Ford revolutionized the world with his implementation of mass production for the Model T automobile. Gain valuable business insight into his life and work with his own auto-biography... "We have only started on our development of our country we have not as yet, with all our talk of wonderful progress, done more than scratch the surface. The progress has been wonderful enough but..."

Biographies/   **ISBN:** *1-59462-198-5*   **Pages:300**
MSRP $21.95

The Art of Cross-Examination
Francis Wellman

QTY

I presume it is the experience of every author, after his first book is published upon an important subject, to be almost overwhelmed with a wealth of ideas and illustrations which could readily have been included in his book, and which to his own mind, at least, seem to make a second edition inevitable. Such certainly was the case with me; and when the first edition had reached its sixth impression in five months, I rejoiced to learn that it seemed to my publishers that the book had met with a sufficiently favorable reception to justify a second and considerably enlarged edition. ..

Reference   ISBN: *1-59462-647-2*

Pages:412

MSRP $19.95

On the Duty of Civil Disobedience
Henry David Thoreau

QTY

Thoreau wrote his famous essay, On the Duty of Civil Disobedience, as a protest against an unjust but popular war and the immoral but popular institution of slave-owning. He did more than write—he declined to pay his taxes, and was hauled off to gaol in consequence. Who can say how much this refusal of his hastened the end of the war and of slavery ?

Law   ISBN: *1-59462-747-9*

Pages:48

MSRP $7.45

Dream Psychology Psychoanalysis for Beginners
Sigmund Freud

QTY

Sigmund Freud, born Sigismund Schlomo Freud (May 6, 1856 - September 23, 1939), was a Jewish-Austrian neurologist and psychiatrist who co-founded the psychoanalytic school of psychology. Freud is best known for his theories of the unconscious mind, especially involving the mechanism of repression; his redefinition of sexual desire as mobile and directed towards a wide variety of objects; and his therapeutic techniques, especially his understanding of transference in the therapeutic relationship and the presumed value of dreams as sources of insight into unconscious desires.

Psychology   ISBN: *1-59462-905-6*

Pages:196

MSRP $15.45

The Miracle of Right Thought
Orison Swett Marden

QTY

Believe with all of your heart that you will do what you were made to do. When the mind has once formed the habit of holding cheerful, happy, prosperous pictures, it will not be easy to form the opposite habit. It does not matter how improbable or how far away this realization may see, or how dark the prospects may be, if we visualize them as best we can, as vividly as possible, hold tenaciously to them and vigorously struggle to attain them, they will gradually become actualized, realized in the life. But a desire, a longing without endeavor, a yearning abandoned or held indifferently will vanish without realization.

Pages:360

Self Help   ISBN: *1-59462-644-8*

MSRP $25.45

The Rosicrucian Cosmo-Conception Mystic Christianity *by Max Heindel*   ISBN: *1-59462-188-8*   **$38.95**
The Rosicrucian Cosmo-conception is not dogmatic, neither does it appeal to any other authority than the reason of the student. It is; not controversial, but is: sent forth in the, hope that it may help to clear...   New Age/Religion Pages 646

Abandonment To Divine Providence *by Jean-Pierre de Caussade*   ISBN: *1-59462-228-0*   **$25.95**
"The Rev. Jean Pierre de Caussade was one of the most remarkable spiritual writers of the Society of Jesus in France in the 18th Century. His death took place at Toulouse in 1751. His works have gone through many editions and have been republished...   Inspirational Religion Pages 400

Mental Chemistry *by Charles Haanel*   ISBN: *1-59462-192-6*   **$23.95**
Mental Chemistry allows the change of material conditions by combining and appropriately utilizing the power of the mind. Much like applied chemistry creates something new and unique out of careful combinations of chemicals the mastery of mental chemistry...   New Age Pages 354

The Letters of Robert Browning and Elizabeth Barret Barrett 1845-1846 vol II   ISBN: *1-59462-193-4*   **$35.95**
by Robert Browning and Elizabeth Barrett   Biographies Pages 596

Gleanings In Genesis (volume I) *by Arthur W. Pink*   ISBN: *1-59462-130-6*   **$27.45**
Appropriately has Genesis been termed "the seed plot of the Bible" for in it we have, in germ form, almost all of the great doctrines which are afterwards fully developed in the books of Scripture which follow...   Religion/Inspirational Pages 420

The Master Key *by L. W. de Laurence*   ISBN: *1-59462-001-6*   **$30.95**
In no branch of human knowledge has there been a more lively increase of the spirit of research during the past few years than in the study of Psychology, Concentration and Mental Discipline. The requests for authentic lessons in Thought Control, Mental Discipline and...   New Age/Business Pages 422

The Lesser Key Of Solomon Goetia *by L. W. de Laurence*   ISBN: *1-59462-092-X*   **$9.95**
This translation of the first book of the "Lernegton" which is now for the first time made accessible to students of Talismanic Magic was done, after careful collation and edition, from numerous Ancient Manuscripts in Hebrew, Latin, and French...   New Age/Occult Pages 92

Rubaiyat Of Omar Khayyam *by Edward Fitzgerald*   ISBN: *1-59462-332-5*   **$13.95**
Edward Fitzgerald, whom the world has already learned, in spite of his own efforts to remain within the shadow of anonymity, to look upon as one of the rarest poets of the century, was born at Bredfield, in Suffolk, on the 31st of March, 1809. He was the third son of John Purcell...   Music Pages 172

Ancient Law *by Henry Maine*   ISBN: *1-59462-128-4*   **$29.95**
The chief object of the following pages is to indicate some of the earliest ideas of mankind, as they are reflected in Ancient Law, and to point out the relation of those ideas to modern thought.   Religiom/History Pages 452

Far-Away Stories *by William J. Locke*   ISBN: *1-59462-129-2*   **$19.45**
"Good wine needs no bush, but a collection of mixed vintages does. And this book is just such a collection. Some of the stories I do not want to remain buried for ever in the museum files of dead magazine-numbers an author's not unpardonable vanity..."   Fiction Pages 272

Life of David Crockett *by David Crockett*   ISBN: *1-59462-250-7*   **$27.45**
"Colonel David Crockett was one of the most remarkable men of the times in which he lived. Born in humble life, but gifted with a strong will, an indomitable courage, and unremitting perseverance...   Biographies/New Age Pages 424

Lip-Reading *by Edward Nitchie*   ISBN: *1-59462-206-X*   **$25.95**
Edward B. Nitchie, founder of the New York School for the Hard of Hearing, now the Nitchie School of Lip-Reading, Inc, wrote "LIP-READING Principles and Practice". The development and perfecting of this meritorious work on lip-reading was an undertaking...   How-to Pages 400

A Handbook of Suggestive Therapeutics, Applied Hypnotism, Psychic Science   ISBN: *1-59462-214-0*   **$24.95**
by Henry Munro   Health/New Age/Health/Self-help Pages 376

A Doll's House: and Two Other Plays *by Henrik Ibsen*   ISBN: *1-59462-112-8*   **$19.95**
Henrik Ibsen created this classic when in revolutionary 1848 Rome. Introducing some striking concepts in playwriting for the realist genre, this play has been studied the world over.   Fiction/Classics/Plays 308

The Light of Asia *by sir Edwin Arnold*   ISBN: *1-59462-204-3*   **$13.95**
In this poetic masterpiece, Edwin Arnold describes the life and teachings of Buddha. The man who was to become known as Buddha to the world was born as Prince Gautama of India but he rejected the worldly riches and abandoned the reigns of power when... Religion/History/Biographies Pages 170

The Complete Works of Guy de Maupassant *by Guy de Maupassant*   ISBN: *1-59462-157-8*   **$16.95**
"For days and days, nights and nights, I had dreamed of that first kiss which was to consecrate our engagement, and I knew not on what spot I should put my lips..."   Fiction/Classics Pages 240

The Art of Cross-Examination *by Francis L. Wellman*   ISBN: *1-59462-309-0*   **$26.95**
Written by a renowned trial lawyer, Wellman imparts his experience and uses case studies to explain how to use psychology to extract desired information through questioning.   How-to/Science/Reference Pages 408

Answered or Unanswered? *by Louisa Vaughan*   ISBN: *1-59462-248-5*   **$10.95**
Miracles of Faith in China   Religion Pages 112

The Edinburgh Lectures on Mental Science (1909) *by Thomas*   ISBN: *1-59462-008-3*   **$11.95**
This book contains the substance of a course of lectures recently given by the writer in the Queen Street Hail, Edinburgh. Its purpose is to indicate the Natural Principles governing the relation between Mental Action and Material Conditions...   New Age/Psychology Pages 148

Ayesha *by H. Rider Haggard*   ISBN: *1-59462-301-5*   **$24.95**
Verily and indeed it is the unexpected that happens! Probably if there was one person upon the earth from whom the Editor of this, and of a certain previous history, did not expect to hear again...   Classics Pages 380

Ayala's Angel *by Anthony Trollope*   ISBN: *1-59462-352-X*   **$29.95**
The two girls were both pretty, but Lucy who was twenty-one who supposed to be simple and comparatively unattractive, whereas Ayala was credited, as her Bombwhat romantic name might show, with poetic charm and a taste for romance. Ayala when her father died was nineteen...   Fiction Pages 484

The American Commonwealth *by James Bryce*   ISBN: *1-59462-286-8*   **$34.45**
An interpretation of American democratic political theory. It examines political mechanics and society from the perspective of Scotsman James Bryce   Politics Pages 572

Stories of the Pilgrims *by Margaret P. Pumphrey*   ISBN: *1-59462-116-0*   **$17.95**
This book explores pilgrims religious oppression in England as well as their escape to Holland and eventual crossing to America on the Mayflower, and their early days in New England...   History Pages 268

QTY

The Fasting Cure *by Sinclair Upton*　　　　　　　　ISBN: *1-59462-222-1*　**$13.95**
In the Cosmopolitan Magazine for May, 1910, and in the Contemporary Review (London) for April, 1910, I published an article dealing with my experiences in fasting. I have written a great many magazine articles, but never one which attracted so much attention... New Age/Self Help/Health Pages 164

Hebrew Astrology *by Sepharial*　　　　　　　　　　ISBN: *1-59462-308-2*　**$13.45**
In these days of advanced thinking it is a matter of common observation that we have left many of the old landmarks behind and that we are now pressing forward to greater heights and to a wider horizon than that which represented the mind-content of our progenitors... Astrology Pages 144

Thought Vibration or The Law of Attraction in the Thought World　ISBN: *1-59462-127-6*　**$12.95**
by William Walker Atkinson Psychology/Religion Pages 144

Optimism *by Helen Keller*　　　　　　　　　　　　ISBN: *1-59462-108-X*　**$15.95**
Helen Keller was blind, deaf, and mute since 19 months old, yet famously learned how to overcome these handicaps, communicate with the world, and spread her lectures promoting optimism. An inspiring read for everyone... Biographies/Inspirational Pages 84

Sara Crewe *by Frances Burnett*　　　　　　　　　ISBN: *1-59462-360-0*　**$9.45**
In the first place, Miss Minchin lived in London. Her home was a large, dull, tall one, in a large, dull square, where all the houses were alike, and all the sparrows were alike, and where all the door-knockers made the same heavy sound... Childrens/Classic Pages 88

The Autobiography of Benjamin Franklin *by Benjamin Franklin*　ISBN: *1-59462-135-7*　**$24.95**
The Autobiography of Benjamin Franklin has probably been more extensively read than any other American historical work, and no other book of its kind has had such ups and downs of fortune. Franklin lived for many years in England, where he was agent... Biographies/History Pages 332

Name	
Email	
Telephone	
Address	
City, State ZIP	

☐ **Credit Card**　　　　　☐ **Check / Money Order**

Credit Card Number	
Expiration Date	
Signature	

Please Mail to:　Book Jungle
　　　　　　　　　PO Box 2226
　　　　　　　　　Champaign, IL 61825
or Fax to:　　　630-214-0564

ORDERING INFORMATION

web: *www.bookjungle.com*
email: *sales@bookjungle.com*
fax: *630-214-0564*
mail: *Book Jungle PO Box 2226 Champaign, IL 61825*
or PayPal *to sales@bookjungle.com*

Please contact us for bulk discounts

DIRECT-ORDER TERMS

**20% Discount if You Order
Two or More Books**
Free Domestic Shipping!
Accepted: Master Card, Visa,
Discover, American Express